My Heart

Leigh Armstrong

Contents

To all of the people who made
"My Heart"
A reality

Thank you!

I dedicate my first book to my friend.
Carol Ann Blunt
1965-2017

Always in my heart!
Wherever this book travels, so will you!

Cover designed by Meg Reid

This book is a work of fiction. Names, characters, places, and incidents either are products of the author's imagination or are used fictitiously. Any resemblance to actual persons, living or dead, events, or locales is entirely coincidental.

Leigh Armstrong
leigharmstrong2018@yahoo.com
https://www.facebook.com/leigharmstrongauthor

Printed in the United States of America

First Printing: Aug 2018

ISBN-978-1-7326939-0-6 paperback

Author Photo by Philip Andrews Photography

Chapter 1

I sit up shaking my head, wondering if that rooster has ever missed a morning. But he hasn't. In fact, he comes to work regularly, gets along with his coworkers, and has been my nemesis for many years. Rubbing my eyes, I toss off the warm covers of my bed because despite rain, sleet, or snow I must be downstairs ready to perform my farm duties on time every day. My dad believes people should work hard for what they get in life—especially his only daughter. I understand, but when I go off to college I will not miss cleaning stalls, feeding pigs, or gathering eggs from the hens. I stand up, take in a deep cleansing breath while walking to my window admiring the wildflowers I've nurtured since I was ten. Nature's way (and mine) of putting calm in the world. I lean out a bit to see my favorite pond, which is one of the best places to put in a boat and get lost in the big blue sky. Let's not forget the healing powers of green grass—the soft feel under bare feet or the vivid green color that brightens everything along with the incredible smell when it's freshly cut. All of this beauty at my fingertips, but I'm ready to experience the concrete world of dorms, classes, parties, and boys.

I make my way over to the mirror taking off my sleep shirt and put on a bra, my tie-dye t-shirt, and pull up the straps to my bib overalls. Not the most flattering, but it works. I head to my bathroom and quickly but thoroughly floss and brush my teeth. My mind wonders to breakfast and what awaits me. Face it, I live for food and I take every opportunity to consume it. Freshman fifteen, I do not fear you!

At the top of the stairs, I'm met with memories of my past hanging on the wall. Grandpa Joe and Nana Beth posing in front of their little white house with their favorite cow, Buttons. I also see my dog Ted with his toy squirrel and then it's the picture of Mom with me. There was a bright sun that day and we sat under the big oak tree out front. I wore a yellow polka dot dress and my mother was in a navy blue one with a big straw hat. We were painting with watercolors, trying to create our next masterpiece. When I saw my dad coming with the camera, I crawled onto her lap. Just looking at the photo I can feel her arms around me. Her hair was short, just starting to come back from the chemo, and blowing like baby duck feathers in the wind. I saw her beauty never the signs of her illness. Amanda Carson Morgan, mother of one curious daughter, Jamie Carson Morgan, played with me no matter what. She had answers to all my questions and called me her "little miracle." She used to have long curly brown hair just like mine and her green eyes sparkled whenever she looked at me. We would play restaurant, rodeo Barbie and make mud pies leaving them on the front steps to cook. She read books over and over at bedtime and we would sneak down to make peanut butter and raspberry jam sandwiches after ten. The disease took her away from me, but she is always in my heart.

I head down the rest of the steps and into the kitchen where I find Ruby wearing a green apron and sporting two oven mitts as she takes a pan of heaven out of the oven. Ruby is a sweet lady who was hired five months after Mom died to cook, clean, and keep me straight. The afternoon I started my period, she sat me down and told me everything about it. I asked her questions about boys and I remember once while hanging out clothes I asked her, "When will my boobs come in?" That one made her laugh and she threw a towel at me.

She catches a glimpse of me before I can surprise her. "Hey sleepyhead, did you forget about today?"

"No. All these wonderful smells mean your special muffins with thick sliced bacon, eggs and cheese. Need I say more?"

I walk into her open arms to receive a warm hug.

"I can't believe you're going to be graduating high school and you are all grown up."

"Please tell me I'm still growing." I look down at my chest.

She smacks me on my bottom. "Little lady, what am I going to do with you?"

"Well, I won't be running into the kitchen grabbing food or walking over your wet floors with muddy boots for a while."

She pauses. "I'll miss you doing all that." She reaches up and touches my braid. "It's been my pleasure to watch you grow into the beautiful young woman before me. Spitting image of your mother."

She then turns her attention to the hot pan wiping her face off with her apron.

I put my arms around her. "Do you know what I will miss when I go away?"

Ruby mumbles. "What?"

"Your strawberry muffins."

Putting her hand on her hip Ruby pushes a plate towards me. "That's what you'll miss, muffins? She shakes her head at me. "Your dad is down with Sam you better get going."

"I almost forgot Sam is leaving for his new home today!" I grab the paper plate and head for the barn. I yell back, "I'll miss you more!"

I eat while running down to the barn. Today, I send my horse Sam to his new home at Covington House where I've volunteered for three summers. They rehabilitate people of all ages using different animals to encourage their progress. I know they'll fall in love with him just like I did.

Dad is standing in front of the stall and as I walk toward him, I can only think how well he fits into this life. My dad, Jamison Craig Morgan, is forty-two years old with skin tanned from long days in the sun. He's wearing his signature brown hat that I could always spot when I was looking for him in a crowd. He's always worked hard, woken up early, and stayed up late, but always found time for me. Teaching me to do the right thing, be kind, and stay true to myself. He disciplined me with a gentle hand, and I learned from every lesson given.

I toss my plate in the trash barrel. "Good morning. I almost forgot about today."

He turns to face me. "Are you going to forget about me when you go to college this fall?"

"Not possible. Just a lot on my mind. I'm here now ready to send my friend off to his new home." I stand by Sam, stroking the hair on his neck. "Remind me why this is the right thing to do."

"You've taken great care of him. Loving him is why you're doing it. He will be with people who need him and will love him as much as you."

I wrap my arms around Dad's waist. "I'm going to miss all your words of wisdom."

His arms tighten around me. "You're an old soul with a good heart and compassion for others. You have a good head on your shoulders and are stronger than you think. Now, are you ready?"

"Yes, we're ready." Pulling out my phone, I snap a picture of Dad, myself, and Sam one last time before loading him into the trailer.

Chapter 2

My high school graduation along, with my 19th birthday is almost here. Long ago, the simple suggestion of holding me back a year to cope with the loss of my mother was the best choice for me. When you are five, you miss your mom, cry and refuse everyone right away. It's a horrible rollercoaster of mixed emotions, soothed only by time and love from those around you.

Small towns offer fewer people to interact with, so friend groups can be limited. Mine is made up of Susan Hadley and Jeffrey Brock. Susan is a blonde haired, blue-eyed girl who is smart, encourages fun, taking chances and flirting. In comparison, I'm still a little awkward, especially with boys and clothes that show my feminine side. Susan says what's on her mind, no matter what, because she thinks its best. We are friends any time of the day and cheerleaders through life's little triumphs lending a shoulder to cry on when needed. I will miss everything about her when we attend different schools in the fall, but our phones will keep us connected.

Jeffrey is a cute and funny guy who Susan found in the lunch line one day and pulled him to our table. Our friendship began over pizza in the cafeteria. She tried to be more than a friend several times but he never reciprocated. Over time he and I developed a quiet unspoken attraction between us, but I felt it would be too complicated, so we've just remained friends. Jeffrey is the guy everyone wants to hang around. He's popular with the deepest blue eyes that mesmerize as he works his charm on you. A little cocky, but never around us. He's tried to get us to play baseball or get up and go running with him many times, which usually ends early with two girl's lying in the grass, dreaming of our futures. When I had chicken pox, he brought me a bouquet of candy bars during a storm. These are the two people who've made my school years memorable.

*

Spanish is my next class of the day but I see Jeffrey standing with a girl, who's all caught up in those blue eyes. I listen to some of their conversation before he spots me. When I can take no more of his game, I finally speak.

"Jeffrey, do you have a minute?"

And there goes his perfect smile as I steal him away. "Of course I do."

The girl, Heather Sims, looks around him to me, then back to him. "Jeffrey? What about later?"

"I'll call you."

She spins around with a growl, leaving us alone.

"I think she expected more. By the way, are you coming to my birthday party?"

"Why do you think I wouldn't come?"

"Because I sometimes say no to your invites."

He walked over to me. "Why is that?"

"You know why."

He crossed his arms over his chest. "You could say yes sometimes."

He moves his hand above my head, leaning on the locker, smiling at me. "Do you remember the pact we made a few years ago at Jim's party?"

"I remember it was silly."

"Let's see…it was Spin the Bottle and we won the last round, which meant our turn would be in his bedroom upstairs, away from all the others for fifteen minutes. We sat across each other on the floor and had a sweet first kiss. What happened next?"

"I stopped you from kissing me again."

"Why?" He lifts my chin. "Please tell me why you would stop fate."

His lips call me now just like back then, but I duck under his arm escaping his hold on me.

"Jamie, tell me the words." He moves towards me.

"Seriously?" He wasn't taking no for an answer, so I begin. "If I, Jamie Morgan, have not had sex with anyone by the end of summer before leaving for college, Jeffrey Brock will be with me for the sake of experience only before entering the gates of college hookups."

"Aww, you remember."

"Yes, of course."

He taps his chest. "I'm here for you."

"I need to go."

He takes my backpack.

"Come on, friend. I'll walk you to class. Your cheeks seem a little flushed, are you feeling well?"

I punch him in his arm and he yelps like it hurt.

Chapter 3

oday is the day 67 students in our senior class graduate from Covington High School. Thank goodness, there was no rooster for me this morning because Dad gave me the day off. The weather is excellent for an outdoor ceremony. I peek out over the crowd, seeing him and Ruby in the audience as I take my seat. After some introductions and a speech or two, my row finally prepares to receive diplomas. I get emotional on my last steps across the stage placing a hand on the picture of my mom in the pocket of my dress, and with the other shake the hand of Principal Baxter. It's bittersweet taking this last walk across the stage, but I hear the whistle sound that Dad uses to find me on the farm when I'm late. It makes me smile as I walk down to my seat. I sit among the others and when the last awards are given out, our caps are thrown, neighbors are hugged and we're released to our proud family members.

I find Dad first and receive the best hug ever. "Dad, we did it!"

"Yes, everything is official now."

Ruby is crying but smiling. "Come here you."

I do as I'm asked gladly. "We promised no more tears."

Susan yells out my name, waving me over to her.

Dad takes the diploma from me. "Go enjoy your friends. This is your day. We'll head back to the house to finalize details for tonight's party."

"Are you sure?"

"Yes."

I join the others as we take our traditional walk through town to the ice cream store for free milkshakes. One benefit of a small town and my stomach!

*

My room is covered with clothes from Susan's overnight bag and the music is pushing our mood into high gear as I come out of the bathroom. She's singing into the mirror, applying her lipstick when our eyes meet. "That's what you're wearing?"

"Yeah, why?"

She faces me. "This is your party. Please wear the dress we bought at the mall."

"It's too revealing."

"We purchased the little cardigan, remember?"

"Yes."

"So put it on, because *someone* needs to see you wear it."

I shake my head. "We're..."

"Friends? A status I hope will change before you both leave for school. Why are you stopping the inevitable? Both of you are into each other—everyone can see that, except you."

"Alright. I'll change."

"Good girl." She talks loud while I change. "Girl, you're always hiding in jeans and t-shirts. Clothes are meant to enhance your girly assets."

I walk out.

Her face lights up. "Oh shit!"

"Too much?"

"You look great."

I pull at the material as she puts her hands around me, grabbing my chest.

"Yep, your boobs are bigger!"

I start laughing. "Finally!"

"Grab the power of being a girl, because a daring red halter dress screams sexy!" Susan squeals.

"Oh, wait, I brought you a present."

"What is it?"

"Liquid Courage." She pours us two small cups of vodka from the bottle. "To us. To a relationship that will last forever."

*

Upon our arrival at the tent, we see other kids dressed to impress tonight. Susan's wearing a short, black denim skirt with a yellow off the shoulder shirt that turns heads immediately. The lights are hung, music is pumping, and the smell of food lingers in the air.

Dad steps up next to us. "What are you ladies waiting for?"

Susan decides to exit, excusing herself to the food table.

"Dad, our farm was the best choice for tonight's celebration. Elise and Mr. Green made this tent simply magical."

"I wanted you kids to have a night to remember. They both will be around tonight if you need anything."

"You're not staying?"

"No, I think I'll read in the quiet of my study."

"Do you feel okay?"

"You worry too much. Don't hide under the sweater because of me it's a pretty dress."

"I won't."

"It's time for me to let you go."

"Just let go a little. I love you, Dad."

"I love you too, sweet pea. Now go have fun."

He turns around, hands in his front pockets, and takes long strides towards the house. I follow my father's signature hat until the night takes him out of my sight.

Susan is quick to pull off my protective layer. "Now let's start the fun!"

She pulls me onto the wooden platform, getting lost in the music. We're approached by a couple of guys who want to dance, but who have never spoken to me before. Amazing what the right dress will do.

The air in the tent is a little warm, so I head over in search of water. Jeffrey is standing by the table wearing khaki pants and a blue button up, smiling back at me. He makes a circle motion with his finger. As I comply, he hands me a bottle of water.

"Can you get any prettier than you are right now?"

I turn up the bottle, almost choking on the water. "Come on, Mr. Smooth, let's dance."

*

About midnight, someone shouts, "Skinny dipping!"

Susan grabs my arm pulling me along with the others.

"Wait, what?"

"Time to show what's hidden beneath."

"I can't! What if Dad comes looking for us?"

"I haven't seen him since we started. He's probably asleep in front of the TV."

Susan yanks me down the hill to the pond as kids are jumping in from every direction. She peels off her clothing in no time, yanking at mine as I catch the front to keep it from falling down.

Someone laughs next to me. I cut my eyes at Jeffrey. "Don't encourage her bad behavior."

He looks at me. "Want to join in?"

"Maybe. You?"

"Hey, I'm in if you are."

"It looks like fun."

"Then do it."

Peeling off my clothing, I sprint to the water. Out of nowhere, Jeffrey runs past me completely naked, and dives in. After a while, we see flashlights like they are searching for us. Everyone runs out, grabbing clothes, and scattering in different directions.

Jeffrey grabs my arm. "Let's go this way."

We end up at the horse barn, ducking into separate stalls, and pulling on our clothes. I come out wringing my hair as our eyes meet. He walks straight towards me with a look I've not seen before.

"Jamie no more waiting." He kisses me, holding me close to him. My heart is beating faster than normal.

"Jeffrey."

"I like the way you say my name. I always have." We stand still, not wanting to break the moment when he goes to kiss me again but stops. "Please go out on a date with me."

I can't resist anymore. "Okay."

He lifts me up, spinning me around.

"Finally."

Elise, our party planner comes through the door of the barn. "Jamie, thank God I found you. There's an emergency at the house. You need to come quick; it's your dad."

Chapter 4

S ummer's ended and I'm walking in the rain trying to find Apartment 21 at Hopson University— my home for the next four years. I'm glad to be away from Covington, Texas and the farm that will no longer be the same with dad gone. His heart attack, the vigil beside his bed in the hospital and stopping the respirator was the hardest decision of my life. I'm hoping the University will help me to disappear into the mass population of college students. I know what I've lost and the sadness that I feel every minute of every day, but I hope to not show it to anyone while I'm here. The downpour didn't make driving easy and my flip-flops are no match for all the puddles. I look up to see a number 21 on the door in front of me, which I didn't see on my first trip around the complex. After three courageous knocks, the door opens and my eyes fall to a shirtless, sweaty, ripped guy in blue shorts. My guess from the looks of his body, is that he must be an athlete.

"Hi, I'm looking for Michaela."

He leans up against the door, crossing his arms over his chest, displaying the muscles in his arms with no effort at all.

"No Michaela, but I'm Michael."

I take a moment to think. "By any chance is your last name Tucker?"

"It is."

I reach into my back pocket, grabbing the email. "You're not a girl."

A smile crosses his face. "No, I'm not."

I hand the email to him. "Did you advertise a room through the bookstore?" He takes the printed email from me looking at it. "I'm Jamie Morgan."

He looks up from the paper. "You're not a guy."

"No. Clearly there's been an error. Sorry I interrupted you but I'm going to leave."

"Wait, come inside. We can talk it over and you can at least see the place."

Looking back at my truck, my choices at the moment were bleak, so why not? "Sure. I hope your girlfriend won't mind me considering your apartment."

I guess he read through my question, because he answers, "My ex-girlfriend has no say in my decisions and she's out of the country until next semester." He shuts the door. "Let me show you around, but first let me pick up a few things. Covington, Texas, did you drive straight through?"

"Yes, stopping only for fuel. It took me about twelve hours."

"That's a long drive. As you can see, this is the living room/weight room/gaming room. Over here is the kitchen and you're probably wondering about the can and pizza box tower."

"A little."

"We drink and eat tons of pizza, so we thought why not recycle? The money we get back is donated to the no-kill animal shelter in town."

"That's nice and a little unusual."

He smiles. "I guess but I like dogs. Over here is the bedroom for rent which has its own private bathroom. You're soaked let me get you a towel." He leaves then comes back handing me a blue towel.

"Thank you." I hand him an envelope. "This is the deposit, plus first month's rent. If you're fine with renting to a girl, I'll take it."

"I'm good with it." *How do I tell her I wanted her to say yes?* "Welcome home. Are you hungry?"

"Sure."

"How about pizza? Cheese or everything?"

"Everything."

"I'll order it while you get settled."

He leaves and I fall across the bed, staring up at the ceiling. Tears start to form but I wipe them away quickly. No breakdowns to give him a reason to regret his decision. He pops his head back inside as I sit up."

"Do you need help unloading your vehicle?"

"No, all good for tonight."

"I placed the order. You have time to shower because they are always late."

So he thinks I'm a mess? I look down at my clothes. *I am a mess.*

"Did you tour campus before arriving today?"

"Um no. Sight unseen."

"How does one make that choice?"

"Unusual circumstances."

"Want to share?"

"My dad died of a heart attack about three months ago. His lawyer informed me an account was set up here a couple of years back for my four-year attendance. I wanted art school, but he wanted me here for some reason."

"Do you know why?"

"No, and never will. The lawyer gave me no explanation."

"What about your mother?"

"I was five when she passed."

"Wow. Sorry about your parents. I'm sure it's not easy telling a complete stranger about your life but we're roommates, so now it's my turn. I'm into sports from the various bags you see, eating tons of food, working late at night and I don't clean much. My friends are loud frat boys but cool. I have a business driven father, a saint of a mother, and no siblings."

"What's your major?"

"Law."

"I am impressed."

"Don't be. My father wants me to be a contract lawyer for our family business. I'm undecided."

"I saw some funny looking shoes on the floor earlier."

"Rowing. Captain actually. Picture, if you will, a long boat, filled with guys sitting with paddles, rowing to the finish line against other schools. Hopson is serious about their rowing."

"Sounds interesting. Back home it was baseball." I get a sudden chill probably from being soaked from all the rain. "I'm going to take your suggestion and shower."

"No problem. I'll let you know when the pizza arrives."

"Thanks." After twenty minutes of a long hot shower I make my way out to the living room wearing black yoga pants and a yellow t-shirt shaking out my wet hair. I look up as he places the huge pizza box on the table. He also has three choices of canned drinks with bottles of water. As he flips open the top without thinking I step up pulling out a slice and taking a huge bite. I look over at him smiling realizing my inappropriate action.

He smiles. "Pizza's here."

I smile wiping sauce off my chin embarrassed. "Sorry I guess I am hungry. It's really good. How much do I owe you?"

"Nothing. It's a 'Welcome to Hopson' pizza."

"Thank you. Here, let me fix you a plate." I pile two large slices on his plate handing it to him then we sit on the sofa.

"What about the job market on campus?"

"Most are taken by this time, but they'll post tomorrow in McGuire. How old are you?"

"Nineteen. The only experience I have is farm-related, along with helping rehabilitate people recovering from injuries with animals for therapy, and serving spaghetti at the firehouse suppers."

"I play guitar at a bar called '42.' The manager's name is Pete, I'll give you his number."

"That's awesome." I let out a big yawn. "I promise to be more awake tomorrow." I stand, picking up our plates as he follows me to the kitchen.

"I laid sheets over there if you want them."

"Thank you for those and for the pizza, but mostly for letting me stay."

"It's going to be fine. See you in the morning."

*

My alarm is chirping and I wake up to my light on, no sheets on the bed, and boy, did I sleep hard. I begin a mental list of items to buy today while brushing my teeth. I hear the faint sound of music coming from the living room as I throw on my clothes. Picking up my backpack, I open the door to see Michael on the sofa playing the guitar and singing a song when he notices me. He's just as hot in the daylight.

"You're up. How did you sleep?"

"Don't remember falling asleep, so I'd say real well. I have to run some errands before my first class."

He lays down the instrument, jumping over the sofa. "May I walk you out?"

"Sure, if it's no trouble." He disappears down the hall returning in no time.

*

During our walk he points out places to eat outside of the cafeteria, popular student hang outs and a little history of Hopson, then we stop.

"The sidewalk splits into three directions. Go right and you'll find most of your psychology, art, and music classes, plus the gym. To the left are the math, science, business, and law classes. Down the middle are the library, bookstore/cafeteria, and business offices. Can I help you find your first stop?"

19

"No, I think I got it."

"Here's my phone number and your key. Call me about anything. Have a great first day!" Then he jogs away.

Why do I want to call him back? I feel at ease around him. But doing things on my own is what I wanted, what I argued to everyone about the day before I left. Ruby's heart was broken when I pulled away, but we both knew I needed time and space away from Texas. So here goes the first steps to my new life.

*

At the end of my very first day as a college student, I go back to the apartment, dropping bags on the floor to answer my phone. "Hey, Susan."

"Oh my God Jamie, are you okay? Ruby said she heard nothing from you last night, what happened?"

"I'm fine. Last night was interesting and then mix that with exhaustion—I just forgot."

"So tell me about your new roommate. What does she look like?"

"Well 'she' is a guy—6'1, muscular, a third-year student by the name of Michael. He's very nice."

"What? You're sharing an apartment off-campus with a guy?"

"Yes, because of a mix up in the email. But we're giving it a try. He treated me to pizza last night."

"This is fantastic and I'm so jealous. I hope you get to know him real well. Send me a pic as soon as you can."

"He is real cute."

"That's my girl. Oh, I'm so envious of what may become of this newfound relationship."

"Nothing is going to happen—I can't get involved with him. I need to deal with myself, which is one of the reasons why I'm so far away from everyone I know."

"That reminds me. Jeffrey was about to hop a plane to check on you. He's really worried."

"I know he is, but we discussed why I'm doing this."

"I support your decision fully, but he might need time to accept your new need for independence and space. Look I got to go. Love you girl!"

"Love you too, bye."

I drop my head and scroll through my phone to find a pic of Jeffrey. I hear what Susan's saying, but he's better without me. My heart feels empty right now and he deserves a girl who's not emotionally broken. I pick up one of the bags and head to the kitchen to put away the food I bought just as the front door shuts. Michael is holding a new hamper full of items.

"I figured I needed a place to put dirty clothes instead of leaving them all over the apartment. I also picked up two pots, a kitchen utensil set, and these green kitchen towels the lady at the store thought I needed."

"They're pretty."

"Domestication, here I come. How was your first day?"

"All good, except my kickboxing class seems hard."

He raises an eyebrow my direction. "That's really physically demanding. Running, weight lifting, and lots of kicking."

I giggle. "Yes, kicking. Even though the discipline of the program will be a challenge for a nonphysical girl like myself, I feel the need to step outside my comfort zone."

He leans up against the cabinet. "I respect that. My friends will be here at 7:00 and you're welcome to stay and yell at the TV with us."

"Thanks for the invite, but I have a self-guided tour of Hopson tonight. But I bought chips and queso dip to buy their acceptance."

"That will do it."

I grin. "How come you don't live in a fraternity?"

"Do you have time for a story?"

"I do."

"Like any child whose parents give them everything, I was spoiled to the core. 'Reckless' was my middle name and I always seemed to be in trouble. I took many risks and spared no one in my path. My mom found Hopson ranked in the top three for law and it's just far enough away to not fight with my father, but an airplane ride away for her to visit. When I arrived here, I partied hard, putting my grades in jeopardy. That landed me on probation, which angered my father, of course. He in turn donated money to the library but I had to do a few things to keep my tuition. Leave dorm life, stop drinking, and get a job. One day while out running I found the '42' for sale. I negotiated a deal with my father and it was bought six days later, pending some legalities."

"So you own a bar?"

"Yes, a family business. But my bad habits didn't disappear immediately, so I eventually recognized that I was in over my head and needed help. Pete came along looking for a job and something clicked with us. He's an ex-marine who taught me discipline and how to respect a business, which forced me to grow up."

"How was your dad with all of the changes?"

"He never knew I fell several times during the process but I enjoy the business now, even working long hours. And I made a wonderful friend in Pete. Accepting help was never for me but when I did, it opened many possibilities. Now I'm out of a terrible relationship, cleaned up my grades, and drink for fun or when my father is in town. Next time, you have to tell me a story about your life. I'm going to shower before they arrive—do you need help with all this?"

"No almost done."

Did he just suggest I accept help from others?

Chapter 5

*T*onight, I explore my new university, but I'm meeting Michael's friends first. I enter the living room, where I hear voices yelling at the TV. I step up to the sofa and they stop, look at me, and the room goes silent.

"Hi."

They motion different greetings as Michael comes to stand next to me.

"Jamie, these are my shy friends: Ronan, Stan, Kirk, and Jeff."

That's when the fumbling towards me begins as one climbs over the sofa and two run into each other coming around the sofa. One approaches slowly from the left. They all say hi, reaching for my hand at once. After the initial greetings and a few words of welcome, I excuse myself as Michael follows me to the door. I glance back at them still standing looking at us walk away.

"Do you think they'll be okay with me being here?"

"Trust me they like you already. Have a nice tour of campus and I apologize for their weird behavior."

My Heart

Michael

Shutting the door I head to the kitchen for another beer where I'm attacked by my male friend's about my female roommate.

"Dude, this is not fair! Our frat house is full of smelly guys, but you run an ad in the bookstore and a sweet smelling pretty girl accepts. Can she cook? Does she always look that cute? Come on, tell us about her."

"Alright. She's a freshman, first time away from her home in Texas, not bossy or bitchy, and she loves food."

Jeff moves forward. "Is she interested in dating—say one of us?"

"No. Jamie is dealing with the passing of her dad recently, leaving home for the first time and being a freshman. She just needs friends."

Stan slaps my shoulder. "We're just messing with you. She seems nice."

They all go back into the living room, leaving me wondering if I sounded overly protective, like I want her for myself. She's definitely in my head, but I know she just needs time to heal and figure out what she wants for herself. So even I will keep my distance.

*

Jamie

I enter Hopson Cafeteria and I see a tiger dressed in a yellow and blue t-shirt in front of the checkout line. Back home, it was the Racing Cougars, and now I'm a Tiger. In my university guidebook, Hopson University was ranked number three among college cafeterias for good food. I pick fried chicken with a biscuit and green beans, along with a very large slice of chocolate cake. I take a big bite of chicken when I feel someone next to me.

"Jamie?"

With my mouth full, I answer. "Yes."

"Sorry for interrupting."

"You're fine. Caleb, right?"

"Yes, from class this morning. Wow, I'm impressed. Most girls here don't eat food like this."

"I was feeling a little homesick. Have you eaten?"

"Yes. May I sit?"

"Sure."

He pulls out a chair. "What are you up to tonight?"

"A self-guided tour."

He looks out the window, then at me. "I grew up on this campus."

"Really?"

"I live about forty-five minutes south of here. My parents went here and so did my grandfather. My older sister Pamela graduated last year. I'm in McNamara Hall and my roommate's name is Luke. He's from Nebraska and likes to play silent guitar in his underwear all the time."

I giggle at his description. "My roommate plays a real guitar and is pretty good."

"Does she play in the nude, perhaps?"

"Well, she's a guy and no he doesn't. At least not yet. I live in an apartment off-campus."

"Your roommate is a guy and you live off-campus…how did that happen?"

"I made my decision to come here late. No dorm rooms were available. I answered an ad through the bookstore, thinking it was a Michaela, but it turns out Michaela is actually Michael, a third-year student."

"So is he messy and ugly, with a beer gut?"

"No, he's attractive, athletic, charming, and seems easygoing."

"Well you're cute. If it doesn't work out, I could probably fit you in my dorm room. Just a thought."

"I appreciate your offer. Well, I'm pretty full, so this cake will have to wait. Thank you for stopping to say hi."

"You're welcome. I'd really like to show you around campus."

"Are you sure?"

"Yes. Remember, I know the campus like the back of my hand."

"Then let's get started."

After a three hour tour laughing at Caleb's descriptions of the university, I go home to once again sleep soundly.

*

Today is my interview at 42. I put on a pullover grey dress with my cowboy boots, which I hope is appropriate for the interview. The building has two large windows across the front, with some tables outside, and a yellow awning with blue stripes and a lighted sign that reads, '42'. It was 3:55, by my watch, so I'm on time. The walls were filled with sports jerseys, team pictures, and lots of memorabilia from Hopson. There are tables, booths, and a dance area, along with a small stage. The bar is massive, taking up almost the whole side of the room, where many bottles of alcohol are displayed. I turn some more to see Michael walking towards me.

"You're on time. Pete will like that."

"Am I dressed okay? Is he here? Of course he's here. I hope I can do this."

"Wow, you're nervous. Let me find him."

An older gentleman with a buzz cut walks over to us. "Look no further, here I am. You young lady are early." He holds out his hand. "Nice to meet you Jamie."

"Nice to meet you sir. Thank you for seeing me today."

"I was told you're nineteen, is this correct?"

"Yes, sir."

"Does your class schedule allow you to be here Friday at three for training?"

"Yes sir, it does."

"Then I will see you at 3:00 and you'll be trained by one of our best. Are you okay with busing tables?"

"Yes sir. Thank you so much."

"Let me get your Employee Packet and t-shirts. Excuse me."

I could squeeze him, but instead I just silently get excited. "Michael, thank you so much for this opportunity!"

"No problem."

Pete came back and hands me some shirts. "I will see you Friday."

"Yes sir, thank you!" I leave them standing together in the bar as I walk away, basking in the good feeling of landing a job.

*

Michael

Pete sits on a stool at the bar. "How long have you known her?"

"About three days."

"That's all? Because you act like you're smitten by her. Have you developed feelings for her already?"

"What feelings, Pete? I barely know her."

"Well, your face says differently. I saw you watching her during the interview. Will you be here Friday for her first day?"

"Yes, I mean…do you need me to be?"

"She will need you here. Be honest with yourself, she's a pretty girl living in your apartment, and now working in your bar. She seems like a good person with no hidden agendas or after your money. It's good to see you might be falling for a good girl for once."

"Um, thanks."

"You're welcome."

Chapter 6

I dress for my new job, viewing my appearance in the mirror, and hold my hands together, looking up at the ceiling. "Please whatever happens tonight, don't spill anything."

I hear Michael knock on my door. "Do you always talk to yourself?"

"Especially when I'm nervous."

He smiled. "You'll be fine."

"This job is a big deal—I need it to help pay for expenses." I grab my ID, a $20 bill, and my backbone, heading out of the room, stopping just past him. "Wait, are you working tonight?"

"Yes."

"Good." All the way to the 42 I try to calm my nerves and knowing he will be working tonight helps. I step inside as a woman looks in my direction waving me off. "Honey, we don't open until four, come back later."

"I'm Jamie. Today is my first day."

She wipes her hands with a towel. "I wasn't paying attention. Pete told me you were coming. I'm Lacy, official trainer of all newbies. Come, we're going to start in the kitchen. How old are you?"

"Nineteen."

"You read the handbook so no handling of booze because that will have Mr. Tucker losing his license. Understood?"

"Yes ma'am."

"Call me Lacy. The bar can be hectic and you'll be shoved drinks or be asked to deliver, but say no. Tips on the table go into this red basket to be split by everyone at the end of the night. Cleaning the tables, washing dishes, and even doing the laundry have detailed instructions above their stations. Better to learn hands on I always say. Recycling is here for donations later. All of these cabinets, shelves, and drawers are for the busboys/girls and you're the ones assuring our clean inspections. Any questions?"

"Not yet."

"I'm Pete's stepdaughter. Not a student at Hopson, but always learning. I work three days during the week because I'm a traveling nurse. Doors open at four and it's happy hour until six. Don't be scared to weave in between people— politely, of course—to do your job. Lots of fun, but customers can be obnoxious. Next stop, the filling station."

*

She was right. The place filled up fast and the level of noise went up, as did my duties. I move on to a group of tables when I feel a tap on my shoulder.

"Miss, can you come over here? We need booze, shots—can you take our order?"

"Let me find your waitress."

"Why can't you?"

I looked around. "Umm…"

"What's the hold up? Are you okay?"

Panic hits my brain as he moves in close to me, then someone walks by, throwing two bottles in my bucket, which hits a glass and breaks it.

He yells past me. "Damn, dude watch out! Are you okay? What's your name?"

"Jamie."

"Sorry if I sound pushy, I'm just excited. We just received word our grant was approved, so we're over the top, and want to drink the night away. I'm Cody."

"Nice to meet you. This is my first day."

"Well, I need to buy you a drink."

I smile at him. One of the women grabs his arm. "Let's dance."

He shrugs and leaves. I continue clearing, sanitizing, and hunt for the napkin holder. I'm bumped by dancers, overexcited college students taking shots, and someone tries to dance with me, holding the bucket. I blow a fallen piece of hair out of my eyes when I see Michael on my way to the kitchen.

"Jamie how are you doing?"

I let out a little growl then I apologize.

He frowns. "Oh, come with me."

We're at the kitchen sink when he hands me a glass of water. "Drink this."

I do, draining the whole glass.

"You need to stay hydrated and relax; you'll get into the swing of things."

"I feel so…"

"What?"

"Out of place, inexperienced, not tall enough."

He laughs. "Pete has faith in you, so do I. One situation at a time." He fills another glass. "Take a moment to yourself occasionally."

"Thanks for the water and advice. I just want to do a good job." I turn to leave. "Why do I not work more hours?"

"Twenty hours a week, because you're a freshman, and Pete is a big softy who believes in students getting the education they came here to get."

"Good to know."

*

The weeks that followed kept me busy with classes, reading assignments, and a very interesting kickboxing class. I learned to control my body movements, increased my stamina with all the running, along with sculpting my legs, arms, and abs. As for my job, I became stronger and more confident helping out the waitresses while talking to customers. Michael was right; I needed to find my swing. He is an impressive bartender, manager, and a talented singer and guitar player, which he plays at least twice a week. I seem to be distracted by him more and more, but I try and stay focused on why I am here at Hopson. Thanksgiving break is coming up and Caleb asked me to eat lunch with his family. After, I'll return to the apartment to share dinner with Michael. Tonight is Guy's Night and with my paper still to write, I head to the library, but not before stopping for a much needed large coffee. Near the checkout is a group of girls sitting at a table listening to a blonde female who seems to be dominating the conversation. She is wearing a white dress accessorized by chunky gold jewelry while passing around her phone. Stirring my coffee, I listen to their conversation.

The girl in pink: "The place looks so romantic. Explain why you came back so early."

The blonde: "Well, when you spend the money and go through the eligible men, you come home to what's familiar."

The girl in red: "We know who you mean."

The girl in pink: "He has a new female roommate."

The blonde takes her phone back. "Really."

The girl in red: "He was pretty pissed off at what you did. Why do you think he'll want you back?"

The blonde girl: "He has no choice. We're made for each other."

They scoot back their chairs and walk away. I turn to watch them. Could that be Michael's ex? She seems to be very high maintenance and not what I pictured for him. But maybe she is his type. No judgement from me because my experience with boys is zero.

*

I slam the last book shut and head for home. I'm exhausted by the long day, but campus is alive around me. Walking up to the apartment, the blonde from earlier is headed towards me, giving me a once over, then disappearing into the night. As I reach the door, I see an envelope taped to it, with Michael's name written across the front. I pull it off and lift it to my nose. Is that perfume? Who does that? Inside the boys are yelling at the TV and Stan evidently just got knocked to the couch.

"Hey, boys."

Jeff turns to me. "How was the library?"

"Quiet. Michael, I found this on the door for you. I think a tall blonde left it."

He takes it and after reading it, crumples the paper, tossing it in the trash, and heads to the kitchen.

Stan followed. "Do I dare ask?"

"You can. It's from Stacey. She wants to apologize."

Michael takes his beer and walks to the balcony. I watch them all join him out there while I'm left, not knowing the history and feeling out of place. I go to my room and close the door.

Michael

All the guys have left and here I stand, with my hands on the kitchen sink, looking over at Jamie's door. I want to tell her everything, so she'll understand why I threw it away. Jamie asks for nothing from me and when she talks, I want to listen, learning more about her. She has turned my thoughts into clear ones. Of course they are usually about her. I walk past her room to mine and close the door, taking off my shirt and tossing it in the hamper. I like myself better since she moved into the apartment. I don't want Stacey back in my life not now, not ever.

Chapter 7

*D*uring an English Lit study session, Caleb calls with the details of Thanksgiving lunch at his parents' house, which I'm nervous about, but grateful. I kept finding myself reliving past holidays with Dad and Ruby. She would prepare such wonderful meals of turkey, cornbread, dressing and unforgettable pumpkin and cherry pie. When I allow myself to think back, tears start and my heart feels heavy again. I need to focus on establishing new memories and moving forward.

The next day we're on our way to his parents' house as my nerves begin to get the best of me. Caleb lays his hand on mine when he sees me tapping my foot with no music.

"It will be easy, trust me."

We pull up to the house as we see his dad open the front door. "They're pretty obnoxious—almost boring, so don't be nervous."

We walk up towards the house as his dad hugs him, and then playfully places him in a chokehold. His mom gives me a hug, taking me by the hand, and leading me inside where she begins her tour. I see most rooms in the house, four pets, and a table full of baby pics of Caleb and his sister. Definitely a proud momma.

His sister brought her boyfriend and they're cuddled up on the sofa. I catch his parents stealing a kiss or two. We sit down for a huge meal and then proceed to the deck for dessert. When the time comes to leave, both of his parents invite me back, and one of the dogs slips out of the house to follow us. On the ride back, he apologizes for his goofy in love parents and we agree on an upcoming movie on campus and brunch at Dot's next Sunday. I reach over and kiss him on his cheek, then leave to join Michael for Thanksgiving dinner.

When I pull out my key from the door, I can hear yelling coming from inside. I step in, hearing the sound of glass breaking. In the living room, Stacey stands with her hands on Michael's chest, and him gripping her arms, holding her away from him.

"You and I are no longer together! Leave me the hell alone!"

"I can help you. Don't you remember all the plans we made?"

"I forgot everything when you slept with my best friend. I'm done with your manipulations."

They both realize I'm in the room and she yanks her arms away from him, coming over to me.

"So this is your roommate? Sweetie we have more to talk over, can you come back later?"

Before I can answer, he grabs her arm and pulls her towards the door, shoving her out. She goes to speak, but he slams it before she can get a word out. He heads straight for the kitchen, coming back with a broom and dustpan. I stand still, not knowing what to do, but looking at his face and the tight grip he has on the broom, I drop my stuff and bend to help.

"Jamie, you don't need to do this. This is all on me."

I keep my eyes on him. "All I see is someone who got hurt by someone they cared about once and a girl who is not accepting the end result." I place my hand on his and he loosens his grip. "So I'm helping my friend."

We begin to gather the broken pieces.

"I'm sorry you walked in on us fighting. I wanted her to leave before you came back."

"If she didn't pick up on what you were saying, she's crazy."

He sits down, resting his elbows on his knees. "I'm afraid she is."

"How did this all start?"

"My portion of the meal was in the oven and I was getting out plates when I thought you had returned, but it was her standing in the hall. Before I could shove her out, the timer went off and I didn't want it to burn, so I went back into the kitchen. She proceeded to tell me what she wants from me and when you came, she was in the process of being shoved to the door dropping whatever she brought with her."

"How did she get in?"

"I left the door unlocked. Something I won't do again. Enough of that drama. How was Caleb's family?"

"Nice, very sweet, with a spread of food to feed twenty people."

"He likes you, you know."

"We're friends."

"No, I mean he's into you. Like he wants to date or become intimate with you." I look at him with a raised brow. "Jamie that was out of line—it's not what I meant to say."

I nudge him with my foot. "Well, I've never been intimate with anyone." I put my hands over my face. "Oh my God, I can't believe I confessed that out loud! How do you get me to spill things so easily?"

"I got that kind of face. If you want, we can talk about it."

"Of course I'm going to talk about it with you." He smiles. "I was tomboyish growing up, guarding my feelings, and not expressing to boys how I felt. Besides I didn't have boobs, a cute butt, or any flirty moves or confidence to catch their eye. I was awkward and shy."

"What are you saying? We like real girls who are funny, with beautiful smiles and eyes you can get lost in, with big hearts and soft skin." He shoots me a smile, warming me all over.

"There was one boy, Jeffrey Scott. I guess you could say he was my first crush."

"So you dated."

"No. The night of my graduation/birthday party he did see me naked, we shared a body tingling kiss, and promised ourselves a real date."

"Okay, I have so many questions from that statement."

"As the weeks passed after Dad's funeral, I withdrew. He tried to help me but nothing helped me. It's like my heart closed. I cried when I was alone, I took no one with me to see the lawyers, I just withdrew. My parents loved each other but they didn't have enough time together, so I figured I'm doomed to never have love in my life. In the days leading up to my hasty departure I know they all were scared for me to leave, but I needed it for me. I have to discover what I want."

"Do you think about him?"

"I don't allow myself time to think about him. I need to do this for me. You could say it's my own selfish journey."

39

"No, I don't think so. You're human so just cut yourself some slack. You'll figure it all out."

He stood up, taking me with him opening his arms for a hug. I press my ear against his chest listening to every beat of his heart. My arms automatically tightened around him as I gave in to the sweet gesture. His chin rested on the top of my head. I didn't realize until now that I missed being hugged. Out of nowhere, tears started pouring from my eyes onto his shirt. As my little meltdown ended, I stepped away from him wiping my eyes.

"More than you bargained for when you hugged me?"

"No. You needed a hug. This is your home, so cry, scream, play loud music, and bake cookies while eating ice cream. Your journey done on your terms. Then, if you still need a hug, I'm right here."

"You're a good person, Mr. Tucker. I'm going to change my clothes, then we can eat."

"Sounds good."

Michael

I could have stayed in that hug a lot longer. I hope I will be the person she will turn to because she steals a small piece of my heart every time I see her smile, or catch a twinkle of hope in her eyes. But for now I will be her friend in any way that she needs. I can't believe I'm still standing here looking at her door and she's been gone five minutes already. Who knew I could fall this fast.

Chapter 8

Winter break starts in a couple of weeks, but until then I'm preparing for finals. The air is crisp this morning, so my therapy running session should help clear out my head. Thinking back to what Michael said about Caleb liking me, I wonder does Caleb want to take the next step in our friendship? Am I ready for a boyfriend or intimacy? On the other hand, what am I feeling about Michael? I still can't believe I told him about being a virgin. What is wrong with me! I round the fountain and head home to prepare for classes. Later I'll ask Meredith to help me shop for a dress for the holiday party at 42. I see her outside of work and I like her style. She is a third year student, a waitress at work and living on a small budget like myself so she probably knows where to get a nice party dress. I will text her as soon as I get back to the apartment.

At the end of the day, I enter the 42 for my shift and spot Meredith at table 15.

"Hey, do you know a place I can purchase a dress on a tight budget for the party?"

"Yes, there's a little boutique called 'Emma's' on the edge of town. She has good stuff."

"Okay. Next question, will you go with me? I don't pick well and I need an honest eye."

"Sure, we can go Saturday. Wait, Michael's race is at ten, so we can go after that."

"That sounds perfect."

"Last year Pete closed the 42 all afternoon to support them during state competition. We wore t-shirts in support of our boss."

"That was very nice."

"He needed us after what he went through with his ex, Stacey. She's a walking disaster in expensive heels. Have you met her?"

"Yes. I don't think she likes me."

"Well, you live with Michael, the guy she will always want. Let's see. They met in freshman year when he was in his crazy phase. Not sure how she caught his eye, other than she fed his male appetite. He was different back then, especially when he drank. But it all ended one night of her own making and he's better for it. I mean the she-snake slept with his best friend in Michael's apartment. Actually, the room you're in now. The girl has some odd thoughts on commitment because she did it more than once."

"How did he find out?"

"Michael was on stage that night and realized they were both missing. Pete had a family emergency but came in about 10:30, which gave Michael the opportunity to leave. He went home and found them in bed together. He yanked Cliff up and shoved him out the door, along with his no good girlfriend. Cliff transferred schools and she left to study abroad. It all happened this past summer. They were probably done before, because he was cleaning up his act, and she didn't like it when he was sober."

"Meredith, order up."

"Coming. We'll find you something worthy of this cute little body. Let's talk later."

"Sounds good."

My Heart

*

Back home, sitting in my room trying to concentrate on my English paper, I realize I need a break. I grab my glass, heading to the kitchen, when I hear a knock on the door. I look at my watch, puzzled as to who it could be— it's eleven. I make my way over to look out the peephole. Crap, it's Stacey. I wonder what she wants. I turn away, only to be startled by more banging on the door. When I open it, she's standing there in a tight black mini dress holding a bottle of champagne. Her smile disappears when she sees me.

"Is Michael here?"

"No."

"Will he be back soon?"

"Don't know."

"Well I'll wait for him inside."

"You can't."

"I'm not going to wait out here."

"Your choice." I go to close the door but she sticks her foot in it.

"How does a girl like you get into this university? Are you a grant recipient because your parents have no money? Where are you from anyway?"

I look at her foot and she steps back.

"I'll tell him you stopped by. Goodnight." That was too easy. I look out the peep hole and she's truly gone. I must be intimidating in my sweats and hoodie.

Instead of grabbing tea, I reach for a beer, and pop the tab, drinking half of it before stopping. What is wrong with her? I grab the pretzel bag and head back to my room, shutting the door. That is a persistent ex-girlfriend.

I must have fallen asleep, because I woke to a loud noise in the living room. Jumping out of bed, I peek out to see Michael laying on the floor. I go over to him.

"Are you alright, what happened?"

He's smiling. "I tripped over my gym bag."

"Let me help you up." That's when I realized I was just wearing underwear and a camisole.

He paused, looking at my clothes, but I managed to help him up, then moved him over to the sofa where he fell on it. I stood up out of breath.

"Can I get you anything?"

He sits up patting the cushion. "Please sit with me. Stacey found me at the bar, informing me you wouldn't let her inside tonight."

"Was that okay?"

"Yes. I don't want her here."

"Meredith told me what happened between the two of you.

"I apologize for not telling you myself when she came back to town." He leans on his elbows, letting out a sigh, and then smiling at me. "I need you."

What do I say to that? "You need coffee, food, or maybe a bucket?"

"Funny girl. I'm a different person with you here. I like that you have my back and I have yours." He's smiling and his eye lids are getting heavy.

"I think you're ready for sleep."

"I agree."

I lean over him to grab the blanket when I catch a whiff of something strong. "What did you drink?"

"A rainbow of alcohol choices. I tried to remove an evil spirit."

"Take off your shirt." He's smiling again. "Arms up and I'll pull it off. You'll sleep better without it."

Once it's removed and he's covered up, he grabs my wrist. "Thank you, Jamie."

"You're welcome."

I walk to my room, stopping at the door to listen to his breathing. In minutes he's out, so I shut my door, leaning against it. I wonder if he'll remember any of the conversation tomorrow.

Chapter 9

ete is hovering in my office. "Michael, why don't you go home? Everything is finished and you could use a shower."

"I'll go when all the books are finished. My father will want written copies along with computer backup. Which reminds me—what about your report?"

He takes a seat. "All done. Tell me the truth. Do you like running the 42?"

"In the beginning, I wanted two things for myself: access to booze and getting him off my back. What I found was a love for the business, and with your encouragement and support, we have made it."

"I appreciate you including me. You've shown improvement in managerial skills, proved you listen to your employees, and have matured. I am proud of you and you should be proud of what you accomplish here every day. Back in the day, you were an arrogant ass college brat but now you're the conscientious owner of a business."

"Ass?"

"Yes. But someone has taken you further than I could in your transformation. In just a few months of being with her, you smile more."

I lean back in my chair. "She is something."

"That's all you got?"

"We're friends with no pressure, while living in the apartment together."

"If she came to you and expressed an interest in being with you, what would you do?"

"Time will tell."

"Remember, time sometimes bites back. I'm leaving now, don't stay too long. You deserve a break."

"Fifteen more minutes is all I need, then home for a shower."

*

Makeup applied, jewelry on, and now to fasten the hook to the navy blue racerback mini dress. I smooth out the front, then give a twirl with a few dance moves when he passes by my door.

"Did you finish everything?"

"I did. You look nice."

"Meredith turned me on to this little shop out of town."

"You made a good choice."

"Thanks." Then I hear the doorbell. "Caleb's here. I will see you later. Save me a dance." I walk past him to the door opening it to see Caleb standing in a suit looking very cute.

"Jamie you look beautiful."

"Thank you sir. Mighty handsome yourself."

He pulls out a small flask from his pocket. "Limits or no limits?"

"What's in there?"

"Tequila."

"I've not tried Tequila but I choose no limits tonight!"

*

The bar had been transformed into a winter oasis. There was a team to cook, decorate, and tend bar. Girls were in flirty dresses and boys in suits. Who knows where this evening might take us? Meredith heads straight for me waving her arms.

"We made an excellent decision with this one. You look fantastic."

"Thank you for your help. Your choice for this red dress was perfect."

"Yeah, it makes me flirty and fabulous!" She slaps Caleb on the back. "Show her off, and easy on the booze. As for you, my friend, drink water. That liquor will creep up on you."

*

After talking with friends, we sip on the flask, and head for the dance floor. Several songs later, we are both thirsty and in search of water.

I see Michael sitting at the bar in an eye catching black suit. He is unshaven, drinking a beer, surrounded by attractive girls. Caleb requests two waters and I touch Michael's shoulder.

"Hey, you. The bar is over the top tonight. Well done, boss."

Caleb moves next to me, placing his hand on my hip. "Yes, great job man."

Michael looks at Caleb, then at me. "Are you drinking tequila?"

"Yes, just a little."

"Don't worry Michael, I got her tonight." Caleb bends, kissing me, and I'm a little shocked because when it ends, I'm staring at him. "I've wanted to do that for a long time."

He takes my hand, pulling me away from the bar. "I hope that was okay. I know we've never really kissed before."

"Yes, it was fine."

"Well, I'll have to do better next time because fine won't do."

I smile and suggest food, as I begin to start overthinking that sweet short kiss. I need more to drink. I toss back the flask, hoping to relax and maybe see where this night will take me. We eat a little then go out to dance song after song. We have another sip or two and now I'm beginning to feel mellow and warm as my head feels funny. I excuse myself from the group for the restroom. A girl is already waiting, so I stand next to her, leaning against the wall closing my eyes as things begin to spin.

"Are you okay? You can go before me."

"No, I'm fine." I turn to see about eight more girls coming our way. The girl to my right steps in as five leave the bathroom. I never understood the girl-to-bathroom ratio.

I spot Michael with two of his team mates standing by the kitchen when he sees me. He excuses himself walking over to me. I blink trying to clear my vision.

"You're in the wrong line boss," I tease.

"I'm heading upstairs, you can come with me."

"I can't."

"You can use the bathroom in my office." He places a hand on my back, leading me to the steps, which gives the girls in line a chance to cheer and clap for me.

He goes up first, then I follow, stumbling on the first two steps, giggling all the while. He holds out his hand.

"Let me help you."

I take the rest without any problems, cheering internally that I made it to the top. His office houses a wooden desk covered in ledgers, a few filing cabinets, and two computers. I walk over to the only open door, shutting it behind me. I first check my appearance and see red cheeks mixed with lazy, shiny eyes, which means I'm tipsy. I pee, then proceed to wash my hands and fuss next with my hair. I return to find him sitting behind his desk.

"What are you doing?"

He stood. "Waiting for you, did you forget where you are?"

"No, that's silly."

"Here you might want this," he says, handing me a bottle of water, which I down in no time flat.

"How are you feeling?"

"Good." I sit on the corner of his desk. "Why aren't you with that girl? The one with the cleavage bearing outfit?"

"Taking care of you."

"Oh, well I'll go, so you can get back to her."

"No hurry. You can take a seat if you want."

"Caleb doesn't know where I am, so I should grow." I snicker. "I mean go."

"He's trying to get you drunk."

I frown at him. "I agreed to the tequila, no limits tonight."

"Are you ready for anything?"

I look over at him. "I'm not sure. He's sweet, cute, and when he kisses me it's good. But you know how I overthink when I should just do." I hop off the desk.

"Jamie."

I reach the handle of the door when his hand covers mine to stop me. I feel the warmth of his hand, the muscle in his arm pressed against mine, and the smell of his cologne. He's very intoxicating to my senses right now. Kiss him or not? I could just do it and blame it on the booze. I did say no limits tonight. The room seems to be closing in on me. I place my hand over his. "I need to go." I step out flashing him a half confident smile then turn to the steps. Reaching the bottom step I begin to worry about what I almost did, when I run into Caleb.

Michael comes down the steps looking a little intense.

"Where did you go? Caleb looks past me. "Should I be concerned?"

I take his hand to the dance floor. "No, of course not."

Michael follows us out, asking me to dance with him. I nod okay and Caleb steps off to the side. Placing me in his arms, my body starts reacting oddly towards him. *Where is this coming from?*

"I'm sorry for questioning your choices. He's a good guy."

I feel Michael's hand on my lower back holding me close. "I understand. You do know a lot more about me than Caleb. I appreciate your concern."

The song stops but he doesn't let me go. *Is he feeling something too? Am I imagining all of this?*

"Caleb is waiting for you." He lets go, then disappears into the crowd.

What just happened? I find Caleb. "Can we leave?"

"Yes, are you alright did he say something?"

I shake my head, knowing I need air and separation from the guy who is turning my thoughts into mush just by touching me. Maybe tequila is too much.

Caleb walks me home as I try to clear my head about my feelings towards Michael. I listen to him tell me about his upcoming trip to his grandparents for winter break. As I put my key in the lock and open the door, I turn to him. Then it happens. His lips are on mine this time with a purpose. I give in, wrapping my arms around his neck. He backs me inside, shutting the door with one hand and the other hand inside my coat.

"I want you." His hands are moving, pulling me even closer to him. I can feel his need for me, but I can't, so I say his name, then again. "Caleb!"

He stops. "Jamie, what's wrong? Am I moving too fast?"

"I'm a virgin!" With that lovely word being said I walk away from him and after a moment he follows.

"I respect that."

"It's not normal nowadays. I'm not normal."

He places his hand on my arm. "You have to be ready. Don't let me or anyone else rush you."

"I'm sorry. I never meant to lead you on. I understand if you want to leave."

He smiles, then kisses me on my cheek. "How about we find a movie and you can fix sandwiches. Jamie its fine I understand."

"Thank you. You can find a movie and I will fix us food."

About three hours later I walk him to the door.

"I realized tonight there might be competition."

"For what?"

"You." He kisses my cheek then walks away.

*

This morning I hope to make amends for my bizarre behavior last night but Michael isn't up. I pick up my coffee cup and walk over to the sliding doors, letting in the cold air, whipping around to a new voice behind me.

"Oh hey, I'm Lauren. I was with Michael last night."

Shock and awe. Say something. "Would you like some coffee?"

"No. Are you Jamie?"

"Yes."

"Nice to meet you. He told me you were his roommate. You're a lucky girl—he's incredible. Well, bye."

He never brings girls home. Why is this weirding me out? I sit down and turn on the TV, just as he comes out of his room, holding his head and squinting from the morning sun.

"Jamie, you're up."

"I am. I just met your friend."

He goes in for coffee, coming out with a bottle of ibuprofen. "Where is Caleb?"

"He left after we watched a movie last night. Nothing physical, just a movie."

He closes his eyes.

"I guess you didn't drink enough water, so maybe I should have worried about you." I got up, needing to leave.

"Jamie please, can we talk?"

"No, it's alright. I just didn't expect her this morning. You can make your own choices without anyone questioning them, just like me." I walk past him to sit down on the far end of the sofa.

"Look, I drank too much and she walked home with me. She stayed because it was late. I apologize about what I said. It's not my place to give advice to you."

Now I feel ridiculous. He has always been protective of me. "You don't owe me an explanation of why she was here. As for last night, I appreciate your concern for me, but I'm not your responsibility."

"I care."

I bump his arm. "I know you do." We sit in silence for a few minutes. "Old man, you look rough. Can I do anything for you?"

"Old man?"

"Yep." I push him over. "A shower might help that hangover."

"Thanks for caring."

"Oh, and some water, maybe food." He tosses a pillow at me as I walk off to the kitchen.

Chapter 10

*A*fter a breakfast of pancakes and sausage, Michael agrees to go along with me to pick out a tree. In a few days I will spend my first Christmas alone with no family or friends. A decision I made for myself, after declining their offers of trips and them having to wonder when I might break down.

Two hours later, we loaded the small evergreen into my truck, but not before devouring mini donuts, a cup of warm apple cider, and pics with Santa. I would say it's a great start so far. We arrive back home so Michael can pack for his trip and I set out to make snowflakes, hang a string of white lights, and cut a successful star out of aluminum. Standing back, marveling at my rustic creation, I hear him coming up the hall.

"Did you make these ornaments while I packed?"

"Some."

"Thanks for today. It was fun even with my hangover."

"A ritual everyone should do at least once in their lifetime."

He reaches over, touching a limb. "As a kid, trees magically appeared fully decorated and in every room. This experience was much better. Thank you."

I look at him then at the tree. "I guess you need to go, so you don't miss your flight."

"You're right. Save me some cookies—I saw the grocery list of ingredients."

"I will. See you in seven days."

After he leaves, I take a bath, paint my toenails a festive red color, and fill my day with chilling on the sofa watching TV while eating whatever I want. I lock up about 11:00, cut off all lights, and settle in my bed. Looking at my family photos, past Christmas memories run through my brain as I sink down in the covers hoping for sleep.

The next day I keep my pajamas on, braid my hair and welcome the morning. I decide on juice first, so I head to the fridge, grabbing the juice bottle from behind the milk. The bottle has a note attached.

Jamie there is a surprise on my bed that comes from a conversation we had a while back.

Enjoy! PS: We need more juice. Merry Christmas, Michael

I walk to his room, curious as a cat, and find a sketchpad with pencils tied up in a green ribbon. He really listens. I go back to the kitchen to send him a text and then eat a big bowl of cereal. Several holiday themed movies and a long nap later, I awake to a dark apartment, startled by loud knocking at my door. Fumbling with the lamp, I make my way to the door and peek out at the person on the other side. Stacey? Why is she here, knowing he's gone? The banging continues even louder than before. I open the door as she pushes past me.

"May I help you?"

"Maybe. I have something for you."

"For me?"

"Are you sick? Because you look sick."

57

I look at my daylong pajama party outfit. "No."

"Oh, I thought the way you were dressed…never mind. Here." She passes me an envelope. "I'm involved in a society of women here on campus,--I'm the president, actually— and we do a lot of volunteering in the community. We're not only about parties. We're about giving to those who need assistance with chores, tutoring, and errands etc."

"Why me?"

"The people we help are down on their luck financially, physically, and need our help. You seem to come from a simple background, which will allow you to communicate with them and let them know we're here for them. Besides, you look like you enjoy working."

Did she just insult me?

"Look it over and come check us out. There is a number to RSVP. This organization can be a game changer for you. Where are you from?"

"Covington, Texas." *Crap why did I tell her.*

She points at the tree. "Does Michael know about that?"

"Yes, he helped pick it out. Do you have holiday plans to leave campus?"

Her arms are crossed as she looks at the tree. "Tomorrow. Was it your idea? He's never had one in the apartment."

"Yes. He told me that and I wanted it."

She whirls around, walking to the door. "I hope you will consider my offer. Happy holidays!"

"Thanks." I shut the door. That was odd.

The next day I begin to sketch, setting myself up on the balcony looking out over the lake. I began my quest to ignite my artistic talent and began drawing the serene scene in front of me. After a few hours I take a break, eating an orange, and pondering the invite from Stacey. The white cardstock embossed in gold trim says:

You are invited to join the Hopson Campus Society of Women, January 12 @ 4:00.

The address was clearly on sorority row, but is it a fancy one or truly like she said? I set it back down and continue my sketch. Pete calls needing help, so I take a last minute shift at 42, and return home about 11:30. I plop down on the sofa, turn on my friend the TV, and slip away only to wake up early the next morning on the sofa. Today I bake cookies. But first, a shower.

*

I sit drinking coffee this morning, wondering if my sleeping marathon is done because today is finally Christmas Eve. I wonder if the weather report will be correct with Hopson receiving two to three inches of snow tonight. How perfect would that be? I look over the package I received from Susan, while enjoying one of many chocolate treats she sent me. I did exactly the same for her: chocolate treats, a Hopson hoodie, and a small stuffed tiger. Ruby forwarded a care package of food—so appreciated! Included were all her own creations: sweet potato biscuits, cherry turnovers, and her famous pumpkin bread with cream cheese frosting. She also sent some handwritten recipes she thought I might enjoy, including her lemon bars. My present to her was a Hopson blanket, along with fudge I made myself. If I was home today, she would be finishing up a mouthwatering meal for us to share at town hall, then we would take a hay ride with our neighbors to church for a play, and then back home to open one special item from each other. But today I create my own tradition. I turn up the music and head to the kitchen to prepare my meal for later.

My day although fun, messy, and delicious was exhausting. I don't know how Ruby did it every year. Instead of milk and decorated sugar cookies after my just devoured meal, I choose wine with gingerbread cookies. Mix that with the movie on TV where the father and son get trapped on the mountain unsure if they will return to witness the birth of the new baby and be with the family for Christmas, I begin to feel tears filling my eyes, as the snow starts to fall outside. Now I'm full-blown crying. Why? What was I thinking? I should have gone home. Being separated from family and friends during the holidays was not the answer. Face it, I was scared about not knowing how I might act. I grab a tissue as my phone vibrates. Michael's picture appears on the screen. I wipe my eyes, taking in some deep breaths before answering.

"Hey, it's snowing here."

"So you like snow?"

I swallow, not to full out sob over the phone. "Yes, I do."

He pauses. "How are things really?"

Pull it together, Jamie. "Good, how are things there?"

"Fine."

"Your voice says different."

"Let's just say my mother has invited single ladies to every party in hopes I will make a love connection."

"Oh, that explains your tone. How did it go?"

"Not well."

"You can explain more when you get back. Let me add to your somber mood: Stacey stopped by."

"What did she want?"

"Me. She dropped off an invitation to an upcoming meeting in January to join her group."

"I wouldn't trust her."

"Well I don't, but they do a lot of good in the community because I looked them up. Do you have big plans tonight?"

"Dinner at my uncle's for about 30 people."

"Well, I should let you get back to your family. Merry Christmas, Michael."

"Merry Christmas, Jamie."

Chapter 11

end the call, knowing she's not doing well, and I'd rather be with her in the apartment when a hand presses on my shoulder.

"Hey, Mom."

"What's wrong, dear?"

"Sorry, my mind is somewhere else."

"You've been out of it since arriving. Why?"

"A girl."

"You're dating?"

"No. Her name is Jamie and she stayed home for the holiday break."

"She's with her family?"

"No."

"I'm a pretty good listener if you want to elaborate."

Without another hesitation, I explode with details of the one person monopolizing my thoughts. When I'm done, my mother just smiles.

"You live with a girl that you've developed feelings for."

"She's unlike anyone I've ever met."

"You like her."

"Yes, but after all she's been through, she needs friends—people to trust. We have a great relationship and I won't be selfish by telling her my feelings while she deals with her own."

She walks in front of me. "Jamie is a lucky girl to have someone to care about her. I think you know what to do right now. I will explain the situation to your father. If I had known, I wouldn't have invited all those girls."

"Well, if anything, it helped me realize what I'm feeling is real."

Jamie

I wake to the scent of chocolate cake or muffins. I sit up in bed with a smile on my face and then my eyes pop open. Wait, I'm alone. I crawl out of bed, grabbing an umbrella next to my door, remembering my phone is on the coffee table. I peek outside to the living room listening to noises from the kitchen. Walking quietly, I trip over a bag, and land on my hip. A person runs out of the kitchen.

"Jamie!"

"Michael?"

"I'm sorry! I dropped them when I came in and you were sleeping. Let me help. Are you hurt?"

"Just embarrassed. Why are you back so early and what is that smell?"

"Come into the kitchen and you'll see then I can explain. When I told my mother about you she had the chef pack up Christmas Breakfast and sent me back to you."

"How did you get a flight?"

"I drove."

"You must be tired."

"I am but this is what you have been smelling. A fresh-from-the-oven full pan of chocolate croissants."

"They are heaven in a pan."

"She also sent lunch, dinner, and a box of brownies. Your voice sounded different on the phone last night. Like you were crying."

"I couldn't hide it huh? It was because I realized being alone was not what I really wanted. I was scared of being an emotional basket case in front of everyone and ruining their holiday. I'm truly happy to see you."

"Well you are not alone anymore. Let's eat."

"What's in the pitcher?"

"Mimosas with cranberry. She thought you might like it."

"Your mother is awesome."

We sit on the floor while listening to each other tell the tales of the last few days apart.

"Oh, I have something for you." I crawl over to the tree and grab the only thing left to open."

He smiles, then tears into the gift. "Guitar picks. Where did you find them?"

"An antique store in town called 'Lilac.' Do you like them? They belonged to Jimmy Hendricks. Story is he was doing a concert at the college and stopped for a bite to eat at 'Artie's Restaurant,' which caused a huge commotion. To make amends he gave Artie the picks for compensation. Artie kept them for years with the story written on an order ticket."

"They are great, thank you. I'll be right back." He comes back with a small box. "This is for you."

"You already gave me a gift."

"This is the real one."

I carefully pull at the blue ribbon and take off the top, revealing a tiny chain with a diamond pendent.

"I hope this compliments the diamond earrings your dad gave you. Besides I owe you big for helping me get my act together since moving in."

I giggle, then pick up my glass. "Here's to good friends."

"To good friends."

Chapter 12

e filled our winter break talking, eating our way through the food delivery menus, and learning more about each other. Running has become a normal part of my day, of our day. He challenges me when we run together, and when I run by myself, its therapy. The "42" is hosting a Red, White & Blue New Year's Eve Bash today, which usually brings in a good crowd from town. I enter, heading to the back. I run into Pete as I'm grabbing my apron.

"Hey."

His arms are filled with boxes. "Happy New Year."

"Happy New Year to you. What's all this?"

"For the party. Are you ready for the massive turnout?"

"Yes, I think so. Point me in the direction I can be most helpful."

"Go ahead and start setting up the tables with all the normal items, then the balloon table arrangements. Over there is a table for party hats, necklaces, blinking lights—all the fun, loud items people can take."

"Got it."

Everyone pitched in and then it was time to go home, dress, and be back for a big party.

*

Unlike the Christmas party, which was by exclusive invites only, this time we worked and anyone could attend. I cleared tables, delivered food, called cabs and sanitized the bathrooms a few times. The night was going smoothly until I noticed who had just blown in. Stacey wore a tight black dress with black thigh high boots and she brought people with her. I see Michael behind the bar stocking beer, just as she makes her way over to him. As he turns to leave, she grabs him in an unexpected hug. Surprised by her, he jerks away, leading her out of the bar area. Why am I so focused on them? He coaxes her out, then the bouncer blocks her path to him. All is done, Michael, one Stacey, zero. Was that her stomping her foot? I guess she thought that if she was nice to me, she'd win him over. Michael leaves from behind the bar, heading upstairs so I follow. The door is cracked open, I knock when I hear, "Not now."

"Michael, its Jamie. Can I come in?"

"Yes, of course."

I find him behind his desk with a glass and bottle sitting next to him. He turns it up.

"I hope I'm not intruding but I saw what happened."

"Yeah, along with everyone else."

"Is there anything I can do?"

He smiles. "No, I just need some time. I'll be down soon.

"Okay." I turn to leave. "She just needs to see you are not available. Maybe then she'll stop trying to win you back. I'll see you downstairs."

*

Michael

>*The door shuts behind Jamie and I push away from my desk. I don't want her to think this is the only way I can deal with my issues. The guy I was with Stacey is not who I am now and I need to work at keeping it that way. I need to find Jamie to explain.*

Jamie

As people wait for their New Year's Eve kiss, I find myself cleaning tables. Is this going to be my year? To let go and find someone? The countdown has begun with everyone cheering, making use of many noisemakers. As the pairing off begins, I rest my bucket on a table when I see Michael coming through the crowd. Stacey gets up from the table as if to meet up with him. Is she serious? This is not going to happen again. What can I do? He's almost right in front of her when I move in, stopping her from reaching him. Face to face I just smile at him as cheering turns into the final countdown.

*

"Jamie?"

I place my hand on his chest. "I'm giving you an out. Do you trust me?"

"Yes."

Stacey is close enough to hear my words. "Happy New Year, handsome!"

I kiss him, a short quick peck. He's in shock. I whisper. *"Kiss me like you want me."* With my eyes, I motion to the left. He picks up on it right away and grins. My world stands still, stops revolving, and all noise is gone, with only the sound of blood pumping through my veins. His lips meet mine

68

with a controlled, deep body-invading kiss. What started as a fun way to prove he was involved escalates quickly into me wanting him to never stop. My hands are around his neck and my body molds to his. He pulls back, rubbing my jaw with his thumb, giving me one last peck, then takes my hand in his.

"Happy New Year to you. Come with me."

Keep it together, Jamie. He was playing the part just like you wanted. Back down your emotions and take in a deep breath. You helped your friend and that's all.

I look back at Stacey, standing with her mouth open, arms crossed over her chest, clearly pissed. Mission accomplished. Michael, two, Stacey, zero. Or is it Jamie one Stacey, zero.

We enter the kitchen slipping out of sight. "I hope I didn't overstep, but I wanted her to think you were not available to her."

"You went out on a limb for me and I'm pretty sure others saw us. Are you okay with possible rumors?"

"If it helps rid you of Miss Fancy Pants, let them talk."

"Then we can address the rumors together. Thanks Jamie."

"You are welcome. I guess I need to get back to the dishes"

I walk out applying lip gloss, then tuck in my loose hair. I glance Stacey's way and clearly she's trying to make sense of what happened. I proceed to do my job but see her leave about ten minutes later. Well played! But what just happened to me?

*

69

Michael

What just happened? I'm standing here thinking about kissing her and how my world has forever changed. How do I not tell her now? A fist hits my arm and I turn to see Pete. "Why did you hit me?"

"What just happened with you two?"

"Jamie was trying to send a message to Stacey."

"That was a bold move on her part. Did you say anything?"

"I can't. Not yet."

"She has changed over the past few months. Waiting might mean someone else will be the one kissing her." He lays a hand on my shoulder. "You're like a son to me and I want the best for you and I'm sure that's Jamie."

Chapter 13

S econd semester starts with a feeling of belonging. This is my home, my school, and I have a group of new friends, one of them Jenny from my history class. She's a go-getter from California, looking to be involved in a club or cause. We decided to attend the meeting of Hopson Campus Society of Women together. The first event is a dressy luncheon to welcome us and receive our assignments that will prove our dedication to the group. Beautiful furnishings, past member pictures, event posters, and awards hung on the walls. The smell of fresh flowers fills the air inside the charming old house. Stacey stands at the front of the room, waving us over. Jenny and I walk towards her as Michael's warnings to be cautious of her motives drum in my ear.

"Jamie, I'm glad you came." Her eyes fall to Jenny. "And you are?"

"Jenny Peterson."

"Nice to meet you. Please, you ladies find a seat because we are about to get started."

I know my eyes were big. Maybe I was frowning, but who was that pleasant individual? Certainly not the pushy person I've encountered recently.

She rings a bell, asking everyone to have a seat. "Welcome to the Hopson Campus Society of Women." After the introduction of officers, detail of accomplishments, and their future goals, it was then explained why we should choose them. Stacey is a good speaker who makes you believe in the purpose of HCSW and their commitment to the community.

*

We ate and as dessert was being delivered they started to pass out new member assignments. When they came to our table, we discovered our act of kindness is helping the Monroe Family, an elderly couple in need of physical assistance on their farm, plus grocery shopping. We sat listening to the details of our assignment.

"Do you accept?"

We looked at one another, all saying, "Yes."

Stacey hands me the folder, telling the three of us there was no time to change clothes and that she needed the final report with their signatures and pictures tonight by 10:00 pm. She leans into the table. "The first assignment is the most important because it proves too us how far you will go and how well you work together."

I offered to drive so we left on our assignment wearing dresses and heels but ready to lend a hand to a couple who needs our help. My GPS took us far out of town to a remote farm at the end of a long tree lined driveway. We began with Jenny grocery shopping, Melissa helping inside the house and I took to the chores in the barn.

*

Meeting the Monroe's made our duties pleasurable. Both were sharing stories of their life and pitching in when they could. With the list finished and Mr. Monroe's signature on the report, we set off back to town. I dropped off Jenny then Melissa and headed to my apartment. My shoes were covered in muck and I wanted to peel my dress off at the door but checked, calling out to Michael to see if I was alone. It doesn't appear he's in, so I peel out of everything, and hit the shower. As I enjoy my peony shower gel, I think back on what we did tonight and feel accomplished. I slip out of the shower, pulling on some boy shorts and a t-shirt to go gather my clothes for the washing machine. Opening the bedroom door, I find I'm not alone anymore, so I grab a robe.

"Hey, guys."

"Jamie, come and grab a beer with us."

"Thanks, but I have reading to finish."

Michael cleared his throat. "Did something happen? It looks like you got out of your clothes in a hurry." His eyebrow went up as Stan and Jeff just smiled.

"Just dirty."

Jeff steps towards me. "This is sounding better and better. What do you mean exactly?"

"I attended a HCSW meeting, receiving my first assignment tonight."

They look at Michael. He just raises his hands in a motion of surrender. "I tried to stop her."

"It was informative and the task was cleaning house, shopping, corralling animals, moving hay bales—things like that in dresses and heels."

Jeff now leaned against the counter. "That sounds hot. Sweaty girls, hay…"

Michael speaks. "I think she was testing you."

"Well if that is true, we all passed."

Jeff held up his beer. "Here's to Jamie for sticking it to Stacey!"

Stan hands me a beer. "You need this."

"Thanks. Hey, what kind of an area is Paxton Heights? Our assignment was there."

Michael tosses his can in the trash. "An area you ladies should not be in at night. That's where she sent you?"

"Yes."

"I knew this would happen. Jamie, you have to be careful."

"I will, but the family was so sweet." I turn and grab my clothes, putting them in the washing machine. Then I head to my room, saying good night as I pass them. I guess I do need to be more cautious when it comes to her. But the volunteering is perfect for me, so I will give it some time.

Chapter 14

ay arrives and my first academic year comes to a close, which I look back on with a smile. I've accomplished many things like securing a job, being on the Dean's List, running almost daily, and actively volunteering in my community. My need for extra money led me to ask Pete for more shifts. Michael is about to leave for a few months, working in the family business as part of an agreement he made when he procured the bar. He has been an intricate part of my growth and happiness here, being a supportive roommate and friend. I find myself wondering sometimes if he would find me to be of girlfriend material, then reality hits and I wake up.

I sit and wait on the balcony while he packs his bag so we can leave for the airport, when the door slides open and with a cup of coffee in hand he asks, "I saw your summer course load—which by the way, seems intense—then Pete said you asked for extra shifts."

I look up at him. "Yes, it's intense, but it will accelerate my graduation date. As for the shifts, I need the money for expenses on the truck."

"So what you're saying to me, is all work, no play this summer."

I stand, slipping my feet into my flip-flops, reaching for my coffee cup. "I'll try and enjoy the summer if you promise to do the same. I've heard you speak on the phone about your schedule, which also seems intense, not to mention the family obligations."

"How did my concern about you turn into your concern for me?"

"I guess our thoughts are on the same path. That's what friends do."

"There is one more thing. Stacey."

I giggle. "Have you ever trusted her?"

"She always did things in an odd way, but I guess I did until she slept with Cliff."

"She's just jealous I live here with you and she doesn't. I'll keep my eye on her, so stop worrying about what she might do to me. We need to leave so you don't miss your flight."

At the airport, I pull up to let him out, dreading his departure. We get out and I wait on the sidewalk as he gathers his bag. He steps close to me, wrapping his arms around me in a giant hug.

"Don't get weirded out, but I'm going to miss your chocolate chip pancakes on Sunday mornings."

I lean in, tightening my arms. "I'll miss your spaghetti on Thursdays." I pull away. "Have a safe trip roomy."

"You have the numbers I left you. Go outside occasionally!"

All I can do is smile, while shaking my head because he knows me too well!

*

Time is flying by and my classes are intense, requiring lots of reading, papers to type, and time spent in the lab. I go to bed thinking of assignments, then wake up to the same. The best part though is that I'm halfway done. I run a few times a week to clear my head and grab food whenever. The weather is perfect but I only enjoy it while sitting on the balcony studying. My communication with Michael dropped due to business trips, onsite issues, and meetings. One of his managers was in a car accident, so he stepped into his job. I assume he hasn't enjoyed the summer much either. I find myself thinking about him in ways I never had. As they say, absence makes the heart grow fonder.

Today I woke up with a foggy brain. My heart is beating faster, like my body is rushing but leaving me behind. The day progresses and the feeling doesn't change. After 2:00, I decide on dry toast to combat the nausea and pop a pain reliever for the headache I now have, then head to class. Hopefully the walk will help calm me down. Two hours later I find myself at the 42 for my shift to find a girl on stage belting out a song. I see myself in the mirror behind the bar. Where is my summer glow? My eyes are still red. Yesterday marked one year Dad has been gone and it was a tough day for me, but that can't be why I feel off today. I move over to the bar to ask Ted for a drink thinking something cold might help my stomach.

*

"Jamie, what can I get you?"

"A ginger ale?"

"Sure. Are you okay?"

I yawn again. "Just tired." He hands me a cup. "Thanks for the drink."

"No problem. There's pizza in the back for us—it might perk you up."

I nod in agreement while walking away. After clocking in, I tie on my apron and grab my bucket, heading to my first table. I have to set it down quickly, leaning on the table to steady myself. I'm dizzy and my chest feels heavy, like I can't catch my breath. What is wrong with me? I look up to see Ted pointing in my direction talking, but I can't make it out. My body just crumbles to the floor and everything goes black. When I open my eyes, Pete is holding my hand.

"You're going to be okay. EMT's are on the way."

*

The next voice I hear is familiar to me, but how could it be?

"Please, my friend, wake up. I need you to talk to me, let me know you are alright."

I force my eyes open. "Susan?"

She puts her hands over her mouth. "Oh my God, you had me so worried." She hugs me.

"What happened?"

"You fainted at work. Michael called me from your phone."

"My phone? How did he know where I was?"

"He's your emergency contact, so the hospital called him first. He was here in no time and has been sitting in that chair waiting for you to wake up. I sent him home for a shower after I arrived."

"How long has it been?"

"You've been out a few days. They say you're dehydrated and you have mono." She hands me a glass of water. "Here, sip this. All you need is rest, fluids, and food. I'm here to help you get back on your feet."

The door opens and a doctor enters along with Michael. He sees I am awake and lets out a sigh, running his hand through his hair. He does look tired but is smiling as he approaches the bed.

"When did you wake up?"

"Just now."

"This is Dr. Fortis. He has been overseeing your care. I was just telling him that Susan and I will be with you to help implement your care at home."

"Hello, Ms. Morgan. You had everyone worried. How do you feel?"

"Tired."

"That's normal. We will be getting you some of our tasty hospital food and maybe a shower just to see how you do. You might be able to go home today if you can handle that and some walking. Now if you two could wait outside, I need to speak with her in private." Susan and Michael left the room.

"Now do you know what happened to you?"

"Before I fainted, I felt dizzy and my chest felt heavy like I couldn't breathe."

"You were very lucky to faint at work. They got you here quickly as your body was shutting down. Dehydration can cause a wealth of problems for your organs. Stack mononucleosis on top of that, and it leaves your body weak and in danger. I will be releasing you with some medications and instructions to be followed to the letter. With the help of your friends and being at home you should recover in no time. A nurse will be in shortly to get you up. Do you have any questions?"

"No sir."

"I'll check back with you after lunch to see how you are."

Susan came back in without Michael.

"Did he leave?"

"No, he's getting your bag from his car. You haven't told him how you feel, have you?"

"We're friends."

"Why won't you let yourself feel something good?"

Just at that moment, a perky tall blonde nurse came in, kicking Susan out for an overall assessment.

After my shower, a tray of liquids awaits me, and I start sipping, pacing myself not to overdo. Michael returns with a bag in hand.

"I brought you some items from home. You look better already."

"The shower was nice. I'm sorry they called you. You've been so busy, I hope it didn't cause a problem."

"Don't be sorry." He lays his hand on mine and starts to say something as Dr. Fortis comes back in.

The doctor looks at my tray. "If you can handle this tray, in a couple hours we'll try food with substance. I can release you this afternoon if your blood test comes back in the normal range. Any lightheadedness, nausea, or pain?"

"No sir."

"Good. Seems someone wants to go home today."

"Yes sir, I do."

Michael reaches out his hand. "Thank you, Dr. Fortis."

"No problem. I will see you later."

Chapter 15

$\mathcal{A}$rriving back at the apartment, I'm helped out of the car by Michael, while Susan retrieves my bag from the back seat. Once inside I'm prompted by both friends to sit on the sofa, which I do without argument. I kick off my flip-flops, then settle onto the sofa. I have to admit I'm getting a little tired and maybe a little hungry. Susan comes around the end of the sofa and bends down close to me. She looks over at him, then back at me.

"I'll put my things in your room and I will freshen up if you want some time with you know who."

With a wink and a smile she's gone. Michael is in the kitchen opening and shutting cabinets, more than I've ever heard before.

"Michael, what are you doing?"

He pops his head through the window separating the two rooms. "I'm taking care of you."

"What does that mean?"

"You'll see. Just give me a second and I'll be right out."

I prop my legs up on the coffee table in hopes that he'll sit beside me. He comes out of the kitchen, holding a tray and frowning.

"What were you eating? I haven't seen the pantry this bare since you moved in. Until I can get to the store to restock, I made you a snack. Here is iced water and a protein bar."

He wants to do the right thing, give me fluids and give me food, but I was about to cry seeing the bare tray and his worry. Here in front of me, is an amazing guy who I am truly lucky to have in my life, but I clearly can't do the one thing he asks of me. I reach up and touch his arm.

"Please sit with me?" Tears are spilling out onto my cheeks as I try to wipe them away. I start sputtering words that I'm sorry, I wish I had done a better job, I felt I let him down. He reaches over, pulling me towards him, locking me in his arms.

"Stop apologizing. You pushed yourself too hard but I know you would do anything to make everything you had going on work. Leaving to come here when you were admitted to the hospital was not even a second thought for me. I wouldn't have it any other way."

I pull away from him. "You've done so much for me since I came to Hopson. You've always been here for me. I don't blame you if you're mad at me."

He takes my hand in his. "The doctor told me over the phone that your organs would start shutting down, if you didn't get the proper treatment. I left the conference, called my father, and asked for the company jet. When I told him what was going on, he agreed I needed to leave. Did you feel yourself getting sick?"

"I felt it the day I passed out."

He looked down at me. "And the extra hours at work?"

"Don't blame Pete, I needed the money."

"So, not much fun for Jamie this summer?"

"You weren't having any fun either. I could tell from your voice over the phone."

He says nothing at first. "You have a protein bar to eat."

"Yes, I do."

Susan comes into the living room and Michael gets up.

"I'm going to make a list for groceries while you two talk."

I pick up the bar and start eating, demolishing it in seconds.

Susan sits on the sofa. She looks at him then back at me smiling. "He is really cute."

"I'm sorry that I can't do much while you are here. Bad timing on my part."

"It's okay. Jamie you work too hard pushing yourself to do it all. You don't have to prove anything to anyone except yourself. Now take a nap and I will go assist Mr. Gorgeous with his list." She leans over, planting a kiss on my head.

I snuggle down in the sofa, falling asleep to the sound of my two best friends discussing food options.

The next couple of hours we catch up while Michael goes to the store coming back with enough food for two weeks. They both put the groceries away, make dinner, and now Susan and I are watching a movie. Michael grabs his keys after being on the phone.

"Jamie, do you need anything?"

"No, I'm fine. You are leaving?"

"Just for a little bit. I talked with Pete and I'm going down to the 42 for a while. He said if I was in town, he could use my help."

"Is everything okay?"

"Yeah, just paperwork issues. Can I bring you back anything?"

"No, but thank you."

He comes over to the sofa. "How about some peach pie?"

I smile, thinking how good Tom's peach pie is. "Oh, pie sounds scrumptious."

"On it. Susan, what about you?"

"Peach pie sounds good."

He pushes his wallet into his back pocket. "I'll see you ladies later."

Susan cranes so hard watching him walk away that she falls into me. "I still don't know why you haven't hit all that yet."

"Once again, friends."

"Hello, but friends with benefits are the best kind of friends."

*

After several days of much needed rest and attention from them, I was eating normally and drinking plenty of liquids. I had a follow up doctor's visit and he said I was doing well. He wanted me home another week. I was itching to get out and enjoy some summer sun, maybe go for a run, but I promised I would not. Susan was leaving tomorrow and I already missed our late night girl talks. Michael would have to go back as well, and then I will be on my own. But this time I would do better and pay attention to what my body needed. But right now, my body is craving some outdoor time. I pop my head into the living room. Michael is on his computer, Susan on her phone.

"Hey guys, how about we go and do something fun down at the lake?" They both shot me a look.

Susan jumps out of her chair, "Count me in!"

Michael lays the computer aside. "Are you sure you're up to it?"

"Yes, I've been a model patient and the both of you need a distraction. Maybe some cheeseburgers on the grill. You could call some of the guys who are in town."

Susan chimes into the begging party. "Unattached guys, I hope."

Michael pulls out his phone. "I'll try my best."

Susan brushes by me, heading for my bedroom. I look back at him. "Thank you."

*

We're standing in the living room ready to go, when he comes out, wearing red trunks with no shirt. Susan hits my arm and I look up. What I saw was all the worry gone from his face that he'd had for the past several days. She pinches me and when I look at her, she's looking at him. I just smile.

"I called a few guys in town. I told them of our plans and they're bringing anyone who is here. Shall we go?"

I poke Susan so she can close her mouth. "Yes."

"Then let's go."

We follow him out the door.

She whispers. "You live with that every day," Then she bites her knuckles.

We arrive at the lake and there are a lot of people already set up. It's perfect—just what we all need.

Susan grabs Michael's arm. "Who's that guy?"

"That's Brody, he just moved here from Nevada."

"Do you know anything about him?"

"Are you looking short term?"

"Yes, I am in the moment."

"Then go, he's cool."

She wraps her arm around my shoulders. "What do you think?"

"He's attractive."

"Jamie, will you be okay if I, um go over to him?"

"Yes, go make friends."

She looks past me at Michael. "I'll be back, keep an eye on her."

I watch my friend peel off her shirt, then her shorts, kicking off her flip-flops and head straight towards Mr. Right Now.

With a quick introduction, she's flirting fiercely, and he's buying all of it. I kick off my flip-flops, and then peel off my t-shirt. I look up towards the sun, close my eyes, and take it all in. I peek over at him.

"Michael, you don't have to sit here with me."

"Are you trying to get rid of me?"

I turn my head to face him, pulling on my sunglasses. "No."

He leans back on the blanket. "Good."

I sit down wrapping my arms around my knees. His eyes are shut, arms above his head tucked underneath, displaying the muscles in his arms as his stomach slowly moves up and down.

It wasn't just the sun warming my skin. I feel warm being near him all the time now. When did my feelings flip and would I tell him?

"How is your dad with you being here and not at work?"

"I told him why I was here. He understood—at least that's what he said."

"I know putting up with the two of us and my illness was probably not what you bargained for your last summer before senior year."

"It's been fun and you needed help. I didn't realize how many shades of blue polish there was or the horrors of bikini waxing until now."

I cover my face, embarrassed. "Okay, you were not supposed to hear that, but yes, it can be tough."

He sits up. "When you're released from the doctor, promise me you will cut your hours back at the bar."

I go to say, "I need the money," but catch the look on his face, so instead I just agree I'll do all the right things to keep him from worrying. I need him to feel good about leaving. I owe him that.

"How about a race to the water and a swim?" I stand waiting for him to do the same.

"How about a walk into the water and maybe a float?"

"Fair enough."

*

I had been terribly spoiled by having them with me. Susan left for her flight and we were both in tears. She made me promise to take it easy, or get laid. A few days later it was Michael's turn to leave. He was moving about the apartment, staying busy not saying much. Finally, he sets his bag by the door and returns to the living room, standing with his hands on his hips, just looking out towards the balcony.

"Okay, you have your instructions for what you can do and what your limits are. You have food—I restocked the pantry. Pete has you on the early shift. No more late nights for the next two weeks. I bought more juice and bottled water. And sleep, remember to sleep."

I get up from the chair, walk over to him, and then wrap my arms around his body, lying my head on his chest. "I'll be fine."

His body relaxes and he rests his chin on my head, letting out a breath.

I lean away from him. "You know, I owe you big for all you've done for me."

"I'll collect my fee when I return."

"I appreciate everything you have done."

We both smile and then he walks to the door. "I'll see you back here in a few weeks."

"Definitely."

*

End of the summer

Michael is due home today, my classes are over, and I'm feeling good. I'm standing on a chair hanging a "Welcome Back" sign, with music playing in the background as I sing along. As I jump off the chair, he walks thru the door. "Michael!"

I run over to him as he drops his bag in anticipation of my hug.

He sets me down. "You look good. How are you feeling?"

"Back to normal. I hope you don't mind, but I planned a welcome back home party."

He sits on the sofa, loosening his tie. "I missed this."

"You missed the sofa?"

He smiles at me. "Among other things."

I nudge him on the arm.

"How did you do with your classes?"

"I passed them all even with the delay of an illness."

"I knew you would."

"How was surfing in California on your mini business trip last week?"

"Large waves and totally the best part of that assignment."

"I'm glad you got to go and have some fun away from the stuffy office scene. You deserved some rest and relaxation. How does it feel to be a senior?"

"No different. Except my dad set up for me to meet with the legal team while I was back home."

"Still hoping you'll change your mind, huh?"

"Probably. What time is the party?"

"About eight. Just a small crowd."

He stands. "I'm going to shower, unless you need me to help."

"No, the sign was the last thing. The guys helped me stock the beer and all the food is ready." He grabs his bag walking down the hall to his room.

"I missed you to Jamie."

Chapter 16

or the past five years on the second Saturday of September, the HCSW holds an auction to raise money for their programs. Tonight is the "Men in Sports Bachelor Event." All the advertising, planning, and phone calls are done. All the captains and co-captains of the sports teams at Hopson are registered. The packets of information are handed out and my attire is to be short, black, and sexy. Not sure if I filled all requirements, but with my black heels on, I left before Michael, arriving one hour before go time. I arrive at the venue where I see lots of shiny stars hanging from the ceiling, twinkling candles, and tables covered in white linen tablecloths. Stacey is standing along with her other officers all in red. She's wearing a tight fitting, mini dress with what looks like glass slippers. Go figure. We gather around them but only she steps forward to speak.

"Listen up everyone. This is the evening we worked so hard to accomplish. Thank you for responding to the many emails, phone calls and meetings over the past few months. Without it, none of this would be possible. We are ready to let people in, but before that happens, the senior committee has an announcement." She pulls out a piece of paper, handing it to Karen, our Vice President.

"All of you in white will work the welcome desk, putting on nametags, ushering guys to the bar and food. Those in black will be escorts.

You are responsible for making them look good, while pumping up the audience to spend money. As for the seniors in red, we mingle. The board put into place the new rule last night when it was brought to our attention the ugly situation last year, so therefore those in black can't bid. Sorry ladies for the last minute change.

No one expected this, so the words that spill out from some were not nice ones. Stacey waves her hands to get everyone quiet then steps up and interjects.

"Calm down and I will explain. Members dressed in black are the closest to our bachelor's before they come out. Trust me, if it were me I would be rubbing some elbows backstage ladies. Therefore, some might think you're working deals, so to keep it fair, this decision had to be made. Let's rally for the real reason why we're here and pull together as sisters." She grabs the microphone. "Megan, open the doors!"

*

The athletes begin trickling in and are met by their future dates along with many female students. About 20 minutes into the meet and greet, Michael arrives with Jackson, his co-captain. They're both very attractive in their tuxedos and others think so as well. I watch as they make their way through, saying hi. Jackson even kisses two on their cheeks. I move up next to Michael.

"Are you looking for someone special?"

"Uh no. Jamie?"

I frown, looking down at my dress. "What?"

He looks it over but says nothing, just shaking his head, and then an awkward smile comes across his face and he puts his hands in his pockets.

Jackson hits Michael in his side. "What he should say is that you look hot!"

With that, the hair on my arms stands up.

"Are you both ready for all this?"

"No!" Michael exclaims.

I giggle as Jackson hits him in the shoulder. "Finally, he speaks."

Michael develops a serious scowl on his face, looking at his friend. "Jackson, would you excuse us?"

"No problem, I'll grab us a beer. You seem a little uptight."

Michael takes my elbow, leading me to the side, out of the way of traffic. "Can I ask a favor?"

"Sure."

"Bid on me tonight and I will drop $500 in your account."

"I would do that for you but the senior committee made a rule that escorts wearing black can't participate in the auction this year."

"That's bullshit. Why?"

"A certain situation last year. We're to show you off and make everyone spend money. If you're worried about Stacey bidding, Jenny told me she is seeing someone, so maybe she's not interested."

"Who would want to be with her?"

I cut my eyes at him.

"Look, you're a strong, handsome, tall, sexy beast of a man who I've heard many ladies want this evening. You'll be fine. Now, go drink a beer or two and enjoy being wanted by all."

He walks away, just shaking his head at me. He's really worried about this and of course I need an untraceable plan. I have to think fast. Miranda my friend from English 102 last year. This might work after all.

All bachelors are asked to go behind the curtain, stage right with escorts. Julie, the student body president, comes out to begin the event. The first bachelor comes out with his escort and they dance together. She peels him out of his coat and he sells for $250. The next guy picks up his escort, carrying her onto the stage. He reaches into his jacket, presenting her with a flower which she tucks into her hair. He kisses her hand, which melts the audience and he brings in $355. The baseball captain is bought by two girls and goes for $500. They literally jump onto the stage and pull him off. The evening is fully charged with eager ladies spending their summer cash. When it's time for the rowing team, Jackson goes first. He shows off unique dance moves, leaving Ally, his escort, spinning even after his moment is done. He then untucks his shirt from his pants, showing well defined abs. He goes for $500 after a great battle for his attention. Both girls are escorted out by security and the winning bid is awarded to the girls swim team. Let's just say he was more than pleased. Michael is up next, so Julie begins to run down his fact sheet. He's taking in deep breaths, blowing them out and stretching his head side to side, cracking his knuckles.

I place my hand on his arm. "This is a first—are you nervous?"

"I'm unsure about this because in the past I was drunk and didn't care."

"Everyone is doing a great job and so will you."

He looks at me with those big brown eyes and places his hand around mine.

"Teamwork."

"Trust me," I say before I hear, "Give it up ladies, for Michael Tucker!"

We come out from behind the curtain, but the music stops, and we stood looking at each other. When it begins again, it's as if we had just entered a strip club, unlike the songs before us. Julie seems confused by the switch and I look over at Stacey's table. There she sits, sipping wine, smiling up at us. The screen is showing pictures of him like the other bachelors, but his are mostly all bare-chested, partying and she is in some of them. Not the pictures I'd seen at rehearsal. My whole body stiffens. I don't want to go any further, but one look at him makes me muster the will to keep going. I did say trust me.

I squeeze his hand. "We can do this."

He nods in agreement, reaching up to loosen his tie, and taking off his coat. What happened next is a blur, a miracle of the gods, and truly amazing. He leads me into moves and I guess we both channel our inner dancer. We're left winded, shocked at our performance, and the crowd screams, raising their paddles.

He looks at me. "We made that happen."

"We killed it!"

"Yes we did." He picks me up in a hug, setting me down and I go to walk away, but he catches my hand. "We finish as a team."

I smile, but I am nervous about what might happen next.

Julie begins to open the bids. I look over at Stacey as she casually stands up and her arm raises with a paddle to bid on him. I swallow hard, but just then, a service person bumps into her with a tray and she's knocked back down, full of anger and disbelief. In that perfect moment, Miranda yells out $500, then stands in shock as Julie hits her gavel down on the podium.

"Sold to #43. First and only bid out. Congratulations!"

Michael tightens his grip on my hand then blows her a kiss.

Stacey's mouth flies open and then she shoves the waiter out of her way, heading up to the podium to speak with Julie. When she doesn't hear the response she wants, she leaves in a haste.

We begin to walk off the stage when I had to explain. "Those were not the pictures approved during rehearsals."

"I realized that when I saw some were real personal. Thanks for sticking with me. Nice moves by the way."

"I just followed your lead. Now go meet your date."

*

After speaking with Miranda about our date, I go for a much needed drink. Near the back of the room, Stacey is speaking with a guy in a baseball hat. She leans in close to his ear and I'm able to see his face. Caleb? What the hell? He has a beard and seems thinner. I try making my way over to them but I'm stopped by a group of girls heading up front to see more bachelors. What's he doing with her? Could this be the mystery guy that Jamie was talking about and why he hasn't returned any of Jamie's calls? How do I tell her?

*

It's been one week since the auction and today is Michael's very important date with Miranda. He plops down on the end of the sofa, looking at his phone, dressed in shorts and a t-shirt, so I ask. "What's the plan?"

"First stop is the Lake."

"How romantic."

He plucks my bare arm with his fingers.

"Ouch, just saying."

"We'll take a ride in an official Hopson Tigers rowing boat and then we're off to 42 for a behind the scenes tour, some mixology tips, and hot wings.

"You are the right person for such a date."

"She saved me from a horrible fate."

"Yes, she saved you from the clutches of your crazy ex."

He bent, placing his head in his hands. "Don't remind me. What are your plans today?"

"A run, lunch, a nap, and a long, hot bath with lots of bubble therapy."

His phone vibrates. "She's ready to be picked up. Catch you later! Don't shrivel too much."

"I won't. You kids have fun!"

I finish my long soak in the tub and pull on leggings with an oversized shirt, then go to make a cup of green tea. I wrap myself in a sweater and stand in front of the sliding door, facing the lake. Letting the steam from the mug cover my face, my thoughts go to Michael and Miranda. I start to think about what it would be like to be on a date with him. Sneaking glances, flirting, looking into those dark brown eyes. Talking to him about his likes and dislikes and finding out what makes him tick. Then there's the goodnight kiss and the feel of his lips pressed against mine. I sip my hot tea, though maybe it should be cold water.

He's clearly gotten under my skin, as I now find myself stealing glances at him. Or when we bump against each other in the kitchen or play video games, my nerve endings get all whacked out. I won't tell him because I respect the friendship we have. So he needs to go on dates and I need to go on dates, but something keeps us right where we are. So maybe the tides have turned.

I'm looking out at the water when I notice a figure move by one of the trees, smoking a cigarette. He's wearing a cap and a dark jacket and reaches for something on the ground. Binoculars? What are those for? He's now looking up at the apartments. I skirt behind the curtain. This is real weird. Is he looking at me or someone else? I peek out again to see him put out the cigarette and walk up to my building.

Feeling uncomfortable about what I just saw, I head over to the front door to make sure it's locked, but notice a piece of paper laying on the floor. I pick it up and flip it over seeing the words, "Watching You!"

I'm instantly chilled, but look through the peephole to see if anyone is on the other side but no one's there. The door is locked but now I'm freaking out. Is this a prank or is it real? Maybe Stacey is getting real creative and still sore about the auction. Either way it's creepy. I reach for my phone to call campus security. After five minutes or so they knock. I tell them everything I know and hand them the note. They ask a few more questions, do a perimeter check, and go over some safety tips. I ask if anyone has called or complained other than me and I don't like the answer: no. I lock the door when they leave, taking my now room temperature tea to the sofa, where calming down takes a while.

*

"Jamie, wake up."

I open my eyes to see Michael standing next to me.

I scoot to sit up on the sofa. "You're back."

"Campus Security was here—what happened? Are you okay?"

98

I yawn. "I called them after I found the piece of paper at the front door."

"What?"

"The note, the guy outside."

He sits next to me. "Let's start from the beginning."

I give him the full rundown, and he stands, walking to the balcony door looking out.

"You could have called me."

"I didn't want to interrupt you."

I go get a bottle of water, then return to sit in the chair.

"I did what I needed to do and that was to call security. Now, how was your date?"

He still looks worried, but eventually speaks up. "She likes fruity drinks, really hot wings, and admitted she likes to watch guys in rowing boats more than being in a boat. She wants to travel to Europe next year for school."

I'm smiling. "A good date."

He stands. "You're not off the hook yet. I want to know more about what happened tonight."

"I know you do."

*

Since the incident at the apartment, Michael has been close to me but trying not to hover. He's been walking me to class or magically appears when I'm done. Some of it is normal for us, but he seems a little on edge

99

since the incident. The sun was out today, not raining like the past three days, so I decide to sit by the fountain and enjoy an apple before my next class. My phone vibrates, so I search in my backpack to find where I threw it over two hours ago. It's still going off when I answer, but nothing is said. I look at my screen for the number, which is unknown. I hang up. I go to slip it back in my bag when it starts vibrating again. Another unknown? I say, hello, twice. Nothing but silence. I start looking around me to see if someone is playing a joke on me. Still nothing, so I hang up, feeling two calls like this and the note is a little sketchy. Now who's paranoid? This time I sit it next to me. It vibrates again, but it's Michael.

"Hello."

"What's wrong?"

"Nothing, why?"

"I'm coming over."

"Why, wait, where are you?"

Before I can disconnect, he's standing next to me, out of breath. "What's wrong?"

"How do you know something is wrong and why are you out of breath?"

"The look on your face."

"I received a couple of unknown phone calls. People get them sometimes it's no big deal."

"Your situation is different. The guy with binoculars, a note and now unknown callers. Have you gotten them before?"

"Yes, a couple. I understand, but relax on the security detail."

"Campus police said you need to be careful. Jeff was going to follow you to class, but he is running late."

"Are you serious? You involved him?"

"Along with Stan and Ronan. We all want you safe."

I shake my head, knowing I won't win this argument. "I appreciate the concern from all of you, but just turn it down a little."

He takes my apple and takes a huge bite. "Will do. Come on, or you're going to be late for class."

I walk after him and my apple, clearly not winning the discussion, but feeling grateful to have friends who care about me.

Chapter 17

A couple of weeks have gone by with a few unknown calls but no peeping tom. Feeling a little at ease, I move on with my routine and encourage Michael and the guys to do the same. We had inventory at 42 tonight, so we're closing our doors at 10:00. The cooks made pizzas so when the last customer left, we all ate, waiting for instructions. Michael came down with folders in his hand, as Pete began assigning us into teams. This was my first time, so I was paired with Meredith on food detail. Overall, it went quickly.

After all the folders were turned in, everyone left except me and Michael, since we were walking home together. He goes back up to retrieve his things so I wait by the bar. When Pete leaves, I go up to see what's keeping him.

"Michael, come on—it's late and I need a shower badly, so I know you do."

I enter his office only to find him sitting behind the desk with a man holding a gun to his head. The guy is wearing a black jacket and faded blue cap. He must have heard me because he didn't seem surprised to see me.

"Come in and shut the door."

I hesitate and he screams, "DO IT!"

Michael goes to move and the man hits him with the end of the pistol, knocking him back in the chair. He grabs at his head and all I can see is blood dripping through his fingers.

"Okay. What do you want?"

"Are you the only one left? Don't think of lying, because I won't hesitate to shoot either of you."

"Yes, I'm the only one."

"What is your name?"

I swallow. "Jamie."

He's nervous, pacing. "Go over to the safe."

Michael speaks. "Let me do it."

"No, she can. Do you know the number?"

"No."

He pushes the gun at Michael's chest. "Tell her the combination and don't mess up."

I bend down in front of it, but I've never opened it before, so I'm hoping I can on the first try. My hands are trembling. I look back at Michael. "I'm ready."

He aims the gun at me this time. "Tell her the numbers."

"Jamie turn it to the left twice. First number is 16, right once, 32 then left once, 46."

I try the numbers but have no luck. "It didn't work."

"Try again sweetie or I will shoot your boss."

My fear right now has to be second because I can see Michael is in a lot of pain. "Okay. Michael tell me again." I listened to his instructions carefully.

When it opens, the guy reaches inside his coat, throwing me a bag.

"Here fill this up."

When I finish, I stand facing him.

"Bring it to me."

I step towards him and can see Michael's eye was swollen. "You have what you want, please just leave."

"No, I need one more thing from you, Jamie. You are coming with me."

Michael jumps up. "NO!"

The gun is now pointed towards me, as he looks back at Michael. "Sit down. I like her better, so she goes." He looks around the room and finds duct tape on a file cabinet and tosses it at me.

"I want you to put it around his wrist and the arm of the chair. I don't want him notifying anyone before we reach the street. Now move."

I walk over to Michael and lean down to wrap his wrist.

"Jamie, I can't let you go."

He looks bad. I want to help him, but how?

"I will be fine."

On his desk, I spot a ball shaped paperweight. I glance at him, and then back at it. He shakes his head, no.

The guy comes over to me. "Hurry up."

He shoves the gun at my shoulder. As I tear the tape, I see him looking at the bag of money. This is my chance to do something. I reach for the paperweight, then swing as hard as I can, hitting him on the side of his head. He drops the bag, turning away from us and I fall against the wall as Michael jumps past me, tackling the guy. They both fall against stacked boxes of liquor. My head is spinning trying to locate the gun—where is it? I see a 2 x 4 sitting by the door, so I jump over the desk, grab it, then turn to swing and hear a loud noise. There's pain in my leg and Michael yells my name. Then he hits the guy, knocking him to the floor where he lays facedown. Michael falls against the wall.

I drop the board, running to him.

"Jamie, you were shot. Let me see."

"No. I have to get you help." I turn to find the roll of tape under the desk and began to wrap the guy's wrist, then his ankles. I look over at Michael, whose head is against the wall and his eyes are shut.

"No, no, no you have to stay awake. Michael, talk to me."

"You hit him pretty hard with that paperweight."

"I wish it had knocked him out." I turn to find the phone, but it's been pulled out of the wall. "Michael, where's your phone?"

"I'm not sure."

"I'll be right back. My phone is downstairs—stay awake."

Running down the steps to get my phone, all I can think about is Michael and what he looks like. He needs help. The dispatcher has me on the line asking questions as I go over unlocking the door to wait for them. As the first officer enters, I hang up with dispatch and I tell him my name as the dispatcher instructed me to do.

"Jamie, is the shooter still in the building?"

"Yes, he's unconscious in the office at the top of the stairs. He's wearing a black jacket. The owner is also up there, wearing a blue button up shirt. Please hurry, he's hurt."

Two officers go up and one stays behind to speak with me. "Can you state your full name and why you are here?"

"Jamie Morgan, I work here. We had inventory tonight."

"Miss Morgan, you are hurt, please sit down."

"I'm fine." Then I hear an "All Clear" as the stretcher gets taken up the steps.

"We need to assess your injury."

I sit down so an EMT can look at my leg.

"It's nothing."

He turns to the officer. "She's been shot and needs stitches." He begins to pull out gauze and tape.

"Miss Morgan, you need to go to the hospital, but first, can you tell me what happened?"

"The owner, Michael Tucker was being held by a guy with a gun. He made me open the safe giving him money. It's in a black bag." I keep watching for some sign of Michael. Then two officers bring the guy down, slumped over in handcuffs. On the officer's radio I hear they're bringing down Mr. Tucker.

I look around the officer and see them. I want to go to him but I'm held back. I see his head is secure and he's hooked up to a bag of fluids. I slip past the officer to the stretcher, placing my hand on his arm, saying his name. Tears are falling down my cheeks, landing on him, as the reality of what just happened hits me. He lifts his fingers, trying to say something, but his eyes close. They take him out as Pete shows up.

"Pete! How did you find out?"

"On the scanner at my house."

"We need to go to the hospital."

"Jamie did you recognize the guy? Was he a customer?"

"I don't know. We need to call Michael's parents he looks so bad."

"I will do that. What about you?"

I hear Meredith at the front door trying to get in, so I go to the officer who's been helping me. "Officer Daly, she works here."

He motioned for the officer at the door to let her inside.

"Oh my god Jamie are you alright? I was walking home when I heard the sirens. Where is Michael?"

"I'll fill you in, but can you give me a ride to the hospital? Officer Daly do you have what you need from me?"

"Yes, you are cleared to leave, but get your leg looked at."

"I will. Thank you." I look over at Pete.

"Jamie, go, I'll stay."

*

Arriving at the hospital, we go in search of information, starting at the information desk.

"Are you a family member?"

"His roommate."

"What is your name?"

"Jamie Morgan."

She comes from out behind the desk. "The doctor will be out to speak with you soon after the examination is done with Mr. Tucker. In the meantime, your leg needs to be looked at."

I'm brought a wheelchair. "I'm fine, but thank you."

The nurse places a hand on her hip. "You need to sit down, because you're bleeding on my floor."

I reluctantly do as she asks and I am wheeled into an exam room to receive stitches and a shot. The doctor offers me something to help me rest but I refuse it. I'm not going to sleep until I know about Michael's condition.

In the waiting room is Pete, Jeff, Stan, and Kirk, along with some employees from 42 who had heard about the robbery. I notice a doctor coming towards us, hoping he has information.

"Who is here for Mr. Tucker?"

Everyone stands. He flips through the chart. "Ms. Morgan?"

I step closer. "That's me."

"Can we go over here so we can speak alone?"

I look back at all of them. "Please, we're all friends and are concerned about him."

He waits a moment then proceeds. "He's currently asleep. There's a little swelling on his brain, bruising, and he took some hard hits to his shoulder and abdomen. Three cracked ribs along with multiple contusions and he's receiving medicine to keep him asleep so he can heal. We'll monitor him for the next 24 to 48 hours."

Pete asks if we can see him.

"I'll allow one person to go in for five minutes. Tomorrow will be better for visitors as long as the swelling improves. Again, I can't express enough about him resting."

I stand, waiting for Pete to go. He touches my arm. "Jamie, you go. Let him know we're here praying for a fast recovery. He needs to know you're alright."

I follow the doctor as he speaks about keeping him calm and not saying anything to upset him. He opens the door where I find Michael asleep, hooked up to bags of fluids, a monitor to his right, and a bandage around his head. I feel so much right now but I need to let him know I'm alright. I wrap my fingers around his hand.

"Michael, if you can hear me, I'm fine. Everyone is praying for you and a fast recovery. The doctors say you need rest, so I will be right outside waiting for you to wake up."

I place a kiss on his hand, gently squeezing it before leaving the room.

*

It's been a few hours since he was brought into the hospital. I stretch loosening my now tight muscles, then see Pete speaking with an older couple. The woman looks over in our direction. They're met by the doctor as all go down the hall. Jeff sits beside me.

"They're his parents."

"Good, I'm glad they're here."

About 20 minutes later, they come walking back, his dad on the phone. His mom walks beside Pete. She's petite, dressed in a gray pantsuit, with fair skin and brown hair piled up off her neck to fit her small face perfectly. She touches her husband on the arm as she points towards us. He nods and she turns, walking over to us.

"Excuse me. If you're here for Michael and don't know me, I'm his mother, Laura. His father and I want to thank you all for your support of our son. He is lucky to have friends who care so much. He is currently holding his own, resting comfortably and I'll ask that you all go home and get some rest. Pete will notify you when there is a change."

We all stood, looking at each other. Meredith puts her arm around my shoulders. "I know you won't leave. Can I get you anything?"

"No. Thank you for staying and helping me earlier."

"I can come back and sit with you."

"Thank you but I'm fine. I just know I need to stay."

Meredith hugs me then walks away.

Jeff and Stan are leaving as well. Stan grabs my hand. "You have our numbers."

Jeff kisses my cheek. "He's strong. Call when he wakes up."

"I will."

Pete speaks to me before leaving, then Mrs. Tucker comes over as I'm the only one left.

"You must be Jamie."

"Yes, I am.

I hope you don't mind, but I'm staying."

She gives me a sweet motherly smile. "I know you will. He would be upset if I sent you home. Are you doing alright? It was a scary situation and I heard you got shot."

"I was shot in my leg—grazed rather. I have a few stitches."

"Did they give you something to help you sleep?"

"Yes, but I refused it."

"I have a room at the Premier Hotel. Would you like to come back with us and rest?"

"No, I need to be here."

Without another word, she moves to the nurse's station. After a few minutes she returns.

"I made some arrangements for you to shower. Do you know you have blood all over you?"

I looked down. "No."

She holds out her hand. "Come with me. Nurse Pell here is going to take you to a shower and give you scrubs to wear."

"You can call me if you need anything else."

"Thank you." I leave with Pell.

After a crying spell in the shower and cleaning off blood from my skin, I dress and head to the emergency room waiting area. His mom is sitting in a chair, arms crossed, looking at her phone.

"Did something change?"

"No. I wanted to leave you some coffee and a sandwich. Are you sure you don't want to come with me?"

"I'm sure."

"Try and get some rest. He will be asleep for a while."

She turns and leaves, but I want her back. I want stories of him as a child—ones only his mother can tell. The waiting room is busy, so I sit in the corner. After a couple of hours, I go down the hall to see him, hoping I won't get caught by a nurse. I open the door, then go over, pulling a chair next to his bed. It's been hours and I feel he's really asleep now with the medication they gave him. His breathing is steady. I lean my head down on the side of his bed. I whisper to myself not wanting to wake him. *I love you.*

*

I awake to fingers gently moving in my hair and the sun coming through the window. I look up to see Michael smiling. A sigh of relief and a smile takes over my face. "Hey, you."

"How long have you been sitting here?"

"Not sure. Are they aware you're awake?"

"No. I'm enjoying a quiet moment. Besides, you were sleeping."

"How's your head?"

"It hurts."

"Let's call the nurse."

"Not yet." His finger rubs across my hand. "Are you okay? How's the leg?"

112

"A few stitches is all. I met your mom last night."

"What about my father?"

"I saw him, but he left to handle things at 42."

The door opens and a nurse comes in. "Mr. Tucker, nice to see you're up. How do you feel?"

"I have a headache."

"To be expected. I'll page the doctor to get an order for medicine." She cuts her eyes at me, but a smile crosses her face. "Can I get you anything?"

"No ma'am."

She nods, and then leaves the room to return with a doctor as I leave, so they can do their assessment. I close the door behind me when I hear my name.

"Jamie." His mother and father approach his room.

"How is he?"

"His head hurts, but he's smiling."

"That's good." His mom gestures to her husband. "This is Michael's dad, Harrison."

He reaches over to take my hand. He's tall with thick slightly grey hair and is wearing a navy blue suit. "Nice to finally meet you, Ms. Morgan. I'm sorry you had to endure the trauma of the robbery. I heard what you did to try and help our son. I would like to talk more about what you saw—maybe at lunch later?"

"I can make that work. Excuse me."

*

I go to the restroom to freshen up, then head off to the vending machine for coffee. My stomach growls, begging me to eat, but nothing is appealing except a bag of pretzels. I'm sitting when his dad comes down the hall. He stops to speak with a nurse, then comes over to me.

"He's as stubborn as they come." His phone vibrates. "Laura will fill you in, excuse me."

Ten minutes later his mom comes out. "They're going to keep him a day or two more, then he can come home. He was never a fussy child when he was sick, so hopefully he'll be good for you. He wanted me to send you back inside. I'll talk with you later. Go home and get some real sleep."

I smile at her, then head for his room.

"I hear you'll survive?"

He laughs, grabbing his middle. "I hope you don't mind, but I volunteered you to take care of me so they can return home."

"I'm up for the challenge, you know that."

"I do. Nurse Murphy is going to get me breakfast. I'll be fine if you want to go home and sleep."

"Okay. I'll prepare the apartment for your convalescence. Any special request?"

"Tacos."

"You got it. I'm glad you are going to be alright." I leave the room, feeling better knowing he will be home soon.

Michael

A few days have passed since I've left the hospital and Jamie is all set to take over my care. My parents stopped by before going to the airport, but a phone call has Dad out on the balcony. Jamie excuses herself so I have some time with Mom.

"Mom, please sit down."

She sits, taking my hand in hers.

"I'm not going to lie, this one was scary."

"Well I'm fine. I was more afraid of Jamie leaving with him."

"I know you were."

My father walks in the room, putting away his phone.

"Dad any problems with the bar?"

"No, Pete has it under control. I want you to take some time off because the doctor said head injuries can be tricky. I spoke with the Dean and he wishes you a quick recovery notifying all your instructors. Laura, our plane leaves in one hour."

"Alright." She gives me one more hug. "Call us if you two need anything.

*

Jamie

I've been taking care of Michael for a few days and his mom has only called once. It doesn't matter how old your baby is—they're still your baby. His friends came by frequently, usually at mealtime, and in time for a game or two of football. Stacey sent over a "Man Snack Basket" and Michael had me deliver it to the neighbors around the corner not wanting any part of it.

Today, he comes out after his shower, slowly pulling on a shirt, as his body is still sore. I can see bruising from the attack.

"Need help?"

"No, I got it but I'm hungry. How about you?"

"How about a BLT?"

"I'll get the bacon."

"No, you have to rest. I'll bring it over when it's done. Your mail is on the coffee table if you're bored. How is your head?"

"Hurts a little. Just a dull ache."

"Meds are soon. Try leaning your head back and then close your eyes until lunch is ready."

"I will. Hey—if I haven't said it today, thank you."

"You've said it and you're welcome."

Chapter 18

Thanksgiving arrived this year with me needing to go home for the first time in over a year. The lawyer/executor of my dad's estate had something to give me. I make arrangements to stay with Ruby while in Texas and to grab dinner with Susan while she visits her parents over break. Michael wants to pay for me to fly, or at least rent me a car, but I have my trusty little truck to take me home, declaring my big girl status. My bags are sitting by the door but I'm hesitant to leave. Michael comes by, grabbing my bags, and stopping at the door, straight out of the shower smelling so good. Just like in my dream last night and two nights before. The time we've spent together during his recovery has my heart racing whenever I'm near him and it's even harder not to touch him or want to steal a kiss. Yes, my feelings for him have changed, but how do I tell him I want more?

"I cooked enough food to share with others if you want."

"You could stay and eat with me."

"This is the only time I can go. Besides, the lawyer made it sound important."

Michael opens the door and I step outside. I watch him. He seems tense, a little on edge. He catches me looking over at him and smiles, but then frowns.

"Why couldn't he tell you over the phone?"

"He said he has a box of information for me as part of my dad's last wishes. He was such a basic guy that I can't imagine what kind of information awaits me." I open the car door and throw in my backpack. He puts my larger bag in on the passenger side, then shuts the door and comes over to my side.

"Do you have everything you need?"

"Yes.

"You know I could fit in a spontaneous road trip."

"No, you can't. I wish you could, but you can't."

He looks over the top of the truck. "Call when you get there."

"You worry too much."

"Jamie, you're a girl on the road traveling hundreds of miles, alone. I'm going to worry."

I step towards him, placing my hands on his waist. His hands come up to rest on my arms. In that slight movement, something shifts and words come out of me clearly.

"You care about me and I care about you. I like how that feels. There are so many things I need to tell you."

He pulls me into his arms, resting his chin on my head. "I have things to say to you, too. I want more with you."

I lean back to look up at him. "I want more with you."

"So it's true."

"It is. When I get back things will be different between us."

"Then hurry back."

*

I sit in my car looking at Ruby's house. I throw my phone in my bag after texting Michael to let him know I've arrived. I look up in just enough time to see her throw open the front door and come out onto the porch. I get out of my car and run towards her, falling into familiar arms.

"I missed you so much!"

"Let me look at you. Beautiful as ever, but with an extra special something. You're going to tell me all about him, aren't you?

"He's amazing."

"You're blushing. Come on in, I fixed some of your favorites."

She's speaking the truth; the table is laid out with pork chops, mashed potatoes, green peas, and lemon chess pie with a pitcher of sweet iced tea. We eat and spend the next few hours catching up. She informs me about her new job and tells me what her family is up to. When it finally comes time to go to bed, I put on my oversized Hopson T-shirt and climb in under the covers. Ruby comes in, carrying mugs of hot chocolate.

"You don't have to wait on me. Let me help."

"You're here just a few days, so let me spoil you." She sits next to me. "So you're having the conversation when you get back?"

I look down at my cup. "Yes, when I return. I don't know why it's taken me so long to tell him other than I was punishing myself."

Ruby looked confused. "What do you mean?"

"Mom died so young, she missed out on so much. Dad spent many years without the love of his life. Their love story was tragic. I felt destined never to find happiness and if I did it wouldn't last."

"I agree some love stories are short and unexplainable. But sweetheart, you need to get out there and live your life. You can love and you deserve to be loved. Don't let what happened to your parents hold you back."

"I just hope I'm enough for him."

She touches my cheek. "You're just scared. Open your heart to this young man because the only regret in your life would be not to."

I lean over and hug her. "I've missed you Ruby."

*

For the meeting with the lawyer, I choose grey pants and a white blouse with black heels. I hang my coat on the chair at the kitchen table.

"Good morning!" I greet Ruby. "It smells wonderful in here."

"Well, look at you all grown up. Are those heels? Where are your flip flops?"

"Not appropriate for this meeting."

"Here's a cup of coffee and muffins. Now please sit down. You have time."

She's right, so I eat two muffins along with an orange. I arrive at the lawyer's office with five minutes to spare. It's exactly as I remember, with an old large wooden desk, a bookcase full of books, and chairs trimmed in blue fabric. Mr. Frost comes into the room carrying a box.

"Jamie, it's nice to see you again. How is school?"

"Good. I guess my dad knew what was best for me. I thought all was settled in his estate so what do you have for me?"

"Please sit down. This box is for you, but not until you read this letter."

My Heart

"I don't understand."

He hands it to me. "Your father wanted it like this."

Dear Jamie,

The day we found out about you, I wanted nothing else in the world but to share everything with you. But over the years you taught me so much. My sweet girl, if you are reading this letter, I am sorry, because it means I'm not with you to explain any of what I'm about to tell you. There was a time in my life that I was not the best man for your mom. I traveled miles away from home a couple times during the year to buy cattle and equipment for the farm. On one of those trips I met a woman. She lived a few counties away and we just clicked. It all started so innocently but then led into a three-month affair. Neither of us were strong, so we gave in, acting inappropriately. The guilt of what we had done began to tear at us, so we decided to part ways. I went back to your mom, determined to make our life together better and thanked God every day for her. I found out later that the woman was pregnant with my child. She didn't want to tell her husband about our affair so she made the decision that she would go back to him, letting him believe the baby was his. She said if I ever told your mom or anyone else that I was the father, she would destroy my life. I went home to tell your mother about the woman and the baby but found out that afternoon the cancer had returned. She had to start receiving treatments immediately, so I never told her. I gave up all rights to the child so I could support your mom during her fight hoping she would never find out. She learned about being pregnant with you one month after treatment ended. She was elated; we knew you were our miracle baby. Our lives took off, going to doctor's appointments, hearing your heartbeat, watching her belly grow, and then you arrived. All pink with brown fuzz on your head and our hope for the future. A couple years after you were born, the cancer reappeared. My beautiful wife, your mother, the strongest person I knew fought so hard to live, but was taken from us. When I was diagnosed years later with my heart condition, I

121

tried to be sure you would know how much I loved you every day that I had and now I want to tell you about your sister. I found out she was attending Hopson University, so I made a bold move to pay tuition so you would have to attend, in hopes that you would meet. I know it was a gamble, but one I had to make for you in case I passed before I could tell you that you are not alone. You filled my heart with joy and I was always so proud of you and blessed to have you as my daughter. I made huge mistakes with my life but I know you will do the right thing in yours. I love you.

Forever your father, Jamison Craig Morgan

I can't move. All my emotions from sadness, anger to pity, rush through my body at once.

Mr. Frost has sat down next to me. "Is there anything I can do for you?"

"No. Is this all?"

He's surprised by my calmness.

"I have a box. Inside, you will find a torn piece of paper with the name Melissa Ann. She was born in Argusta, Texas. There's also a crinkled baby picture and a section of a baby blanket with the initials MA.

"Why now?"

"If she's still at Hopson, she'll graduate this year. I saw Ruby in town one day and asked about you. She said you were doing fine and had adjusted to college life. Your dad wanted you to be stronger, knowing his death would be a shock, so he requested giving you some time. If she's truly at Hopson— or even if she's left—you still have a chance to find her. We could hire a private detective to help."

"No, that won't be necessary. If that's all, I'd like to leave."

"Yes, that's all. The box is yours. Jamie, if you need anything else, please let me know."

"Thank you."

*

With box in hand, I leave his office, numb. The air hits my face outside and I start walking, trying to process the letter. I run childhood memories through my brain as I walk away from this information. I see my fearless dad handle a new horse, run a farm, and still have time for me when I needed him. He was always gentle with me when I was hurt, sad, or heartbroken. I remember the feel of his hugs so clearly and how I felt protected, loved. I shake my head, looking up at the sky. A bright yellow sun above me but I still feel a chill. I go back to the law offices, get in my truck, and drive out of town. I stop in front of the cemetery where my parents are buried. I walk the path, seeing my mom's name first, and tears fill my eyes. I hope she never felt neglected or unwanted by him, because she deserved to be loved. My eyes go to the side where his name is and I just stare at it. He kept his secret from me, so why tell me now? I lost the two most important people in my life—no long lost sister will ever replace them. The longer I look at his name, the more my heart feels empty again. Wiping off my face, I turn away, grabbing my phone from my pocket to call Susan when Ruby's number shows up on my screen.

"Hello?"

"Jamie, where are you?"

I look at my watch; it's 5:30.

"Are you alright?"

I pause slightly. "Did you know?"

Now the pause is on her side. "Yes."

"I need a little time."

"I understand."

I hang up the phone wanting to call Michael but he's at practice, so I don't. Instead, I go to Susan's parents' house, needing someone who knew me, knew my childhood, and could help me process everything.

*

I meet her outside the horse barn and she's set up chairs and lit the fire pit. She sees my tearstained face and comes over to hug me. "What happened today?"

"I found out I have a sister." I wave my hand in front of me. "Somewhere out there."

"What are you talking about?"

"I received a letter today that was written by my dad. Telling me about an affair and a baby girl. And here's the clincher: she goes to Hopson!"

"Jamie, your dad was pretty straitlaced. He had an affair?"

"Yep, before I existed."

"Oh shit!"

"Why tell me now? Why not let his secret die with him?" I realize what I just said and start crying again.

Susan hands me a beer. "I am so sorry. I know losing him was hard for you. What are you going to do?"

"Right now, drink lots of beer."

"I'm on it."

We talk for a very long time about my choices in this matter. When all the beer is gone and all the pretzels and pizza are eaten, it's time to turn in.

*

I follow her to the house, stopping in front of the spare room, giggling. She places her hands on my shoulders. "I love you, always have, and always will. Go back and tell that fine man how you feel. Find this girl, don't find her. It's your decision to make."

I wrap her in a huge hug. "I love you and I needed this boozy night."

"Goodnight my friend."

"Goodnight."

I wash my face and brush my teeth, but the bathroom is spinning and my stomach feels like it's about to erupt, so I crawl under the covers. I leave a text for Michael, "I miss you." I fall asleep soon after, but awoke around 2:30, running to the bathroom to throw up my therapy. My phone vibrates on the nightstand so I answer, but get no response. I say hello again, still nothing. I fall back on the bed, dropping my phone on the floor before falling asleep.

The next morning, I wake up with dry mouth, a pounding headache, and an uneasy stomach. Seeing the time, I go to Susan's room looking for a charger for my dead phone. She's passed out, hugging a pillow and snoring. I don't want to wake her, so I decide to head back to Ruby's. I kiss her head. *Goodbye, my friend. I love you.*

*

I enter Ruby's house about 9:30 in the morning to find her in the kitchen. She looks at me as she dries her hands on a towel.

"Are you okay?"

"No. I have a massive hangover. I think I want to go back to school early."

"Are you upset with me?"

"You might have known, but it wasn't your secret to tell." I sit down at the table. "When Dad died, I changed on the inside, which reflected how I treated the people around me. I shut everyone out. All the anger and sadness left me questioning everything. Two parents taken away from me and I literally thought I was cursed to be alone because of something I did. I dealt with those emotions this past year being at Hopson and meeting Michael. I can't change what Dad did or that I have a sister out there. I can only control what I do for me. My heart is open to receive love, and I want to love someone in return. No more being scared or waiting for some terrible event to happen. I do need to ask you a question though."

"What is it?"

"Do you think my mother knew?"

"Sweetie, I knew your parents when they attended church as young kids. I introduced them over a bake sale. I watched them fall in love, get married, and go through rough patches. When you came along, they worked at being good parents, giving you a childhood to remember while living with her disease. Your mother used to say at church that you were her angel, a beautiful miracle. I visited her five days before she passed. She told me Jamison was her rock, the love of her life, but she knew that now her sweet green-eyed baby girl would mend his heart and bring much joy to his life. She had no regrets in her life, no ill thoughts, just love in her heart and peace of mind."

I'm crying all over again. "Ruby, I'm not mad at you. I love you and always will. Thank you for your support and giving me the guidance to know what I want."

Chapter 19

Michael

turn to Jeff. "There is still no word from Jamie. Something's wrong I know it."

Jeff downs his beer. "Stop worrying man, she'll be here. You're just anxious to confess all these feelings you have bottled up inside. I'll never understand why you let her go an entire year without one word you were in to her."

Looking around my apartment I don't recognize a lot of the people here.

"By the way, who are all these people?"

"Fans! Everyone loves the rowing team and it's an excellent way for you to mellow out waiting for your lady and for me to get laid!"

A girl comes by, handing out drinks. "Congratulations on your placement!"

Jackson magically appears. "What's your name, so we can thank you for the drinks?"

"Trish."

Chanting starts for the team and their recent placement. I want nothing to drink but Jeff tips up my glass.

"You're the captain. We do this as a team."

"Fine but no more." I finish it, then place it on the counter, as she hands me one more. "No thanks I'm done."

A girl grabs Jeff to dance and I'm left with Trish not wanting to talk to her but I ask a basic question.

"Are you new to Hopson?"

"No. I go to Community. I'm unfamiliar with rowing, but you guys placed today—that's good, right?"

"It was a close finish."

She touches my arm.

"These are so tight. You must work out a lot."

I nod, not really listening, then look at my phone again, which seems a little blurry.

"Are you looking for someone? Do you have a girlfriend I should be concerned about?"

"She's heading back from Texas. She's real late, so I'm concerned."

"Well she's missing a stellar party."

I squint, then pinch my eyes because now I'm seeing double.

"Are you okay?"

"Excuse me, but I need some air."

At this point, Stan walks by.

"Man I just got here. There was a small mishap at work. Jamie back? I thought you two would be locked in your room already."

"No, and I feel weird. I'm going out for some air."

"Do you want me to come with?"

"No, but have you met Trish?"

I turn him to face her, making my hasty departure. I stand for a few minutes on the balcony but don't feel any better. I check my phone again. *Jamie, where are you?* Maybe I'm rushing her back because I want to talk to her. For the first time in my life, I know what I want and it's her. I go back in to find Stan talking with Trish.

"Hey, I'm not feeling any better. Will you watch over all this and let Jamie know I'm in my room?"

"Sure, do you need to see a doctor or something you look weird?"

"No, I'm going to lie down. No more people in the apartment or the manager will have my ass."

Walking down the hall to my room, my head feels fuzzy, spinning even. I stumble, hitting the wall. I make it to my room, shut the door, and fall onto the bed. My body shuts down and my eyes close.

Chapter 20

Jamie

I arrived in front of the apartment about 2:30 in the morning, exhausted. I slide out and grab my backpack and the bag of food Ruby sent back with me. The walk up to the apartment is quiet, except for some girls lingering outside. They're dressed up wearing high heels and are talking quietly. I know there was a party, but they're a bit overdressed. They spot me and begin walking away. I round the corner running into Stacey.

"Jamie, you're back." She yells past me, "Wait up, bitches."

"Stacey?"

"Sorry you missed the party, because the guys were so playful. Up for anything. It's nice to know they still like having me around. That party was the best—a memorable one for sure! Happy Thanksgiving!"

What was that about? Inside the apartment, I'm even more confused. I find a huge mess of food, bottles, and articles of clothing, along with guys lying on the floor and sofa. Two are sitting at the kitchen bar, talking. I walk in placing the food on the counter.

"Hey, what's going on?"

"We're discussing the events of last night. A shitload of drinking, dancing, and hookups all over. Truly an epic party!"

"Are you guys on the rowing team this year?"

"Yes. I'm Beau and this is Jared. We're twins from CSU, new transfers. And you are?"

"Jamie. I live here. Where's Michael?"

"Um, we're not sure. In fact, our captain and co-captain have been missing for hours. A bunch of hot girls came in with awesome drinks begging us to drink them, dance with them, and well you know."

"I'll go check his room."

"Cool. If we can't get these guys up, can they stay?"

"They're okay, right?"

"They're still breathing."

"Good to know."

*

I walk around a couple of guys on the floor, shirtless, and two without pants. I knock on his door, but nothing. Do I go in? What if he's with someone? *Just do it.* I turn the knob slowly, so as not to disturb him. The light is on in the bathroom and he is in the bed. He's naked with one leg hooked over the sheet, lying on his back. The comforter is off his bed, thrown on the floor along with a pillow. One nightstand is missing a lamp. I go over to him.

"Michael."

He moves slightly, blinking. "Jamie?"

He goes to sit up, but grabs his head. "When did you get here? I was worried about you. I called and sent texts."

"Michael, there are guys all over the living room and hall, beer bottles, trash, and a bunch of girls just left the apartment, including Stacey."

He sits up, realizing he's naked under the sheet. "What the hell? Where are my clothes?"

"You have no recollection of taking them off?"

"No."

I sit down beside him. "So you came in, ripped all the stuff off your bed, knocked over the lamp, stripped off your clothes, then crawled into bed with an apartment full of people."

He looks around, confused. "No, I came in here because I was sick, my vision was off."

"Were you alone?" Then the look I was dreading. *Did he sleep with someone?*

I can't bear the thought, but it would be my fault for not telling him how I was feeling or that I wanted more with him sooner. I stand to leave, but step on a woman's top. Now I'm nauseous.

"Jamie, please don't go. Let me get dressed so we can talk."

"I'm tired. You owe me no explanation."

I see a program from trials lying on the chair with words written in red lipstick. He's up now, wrapping the sheet around him. I read the words out loud. **"Thanks for the delicious time! Your best girls."**

I turn, handing it to him. "This might help."

I hurry to my room, not wanting to hear his voice asking me to stay. I slam the door, then lock it for the first time since moving into the apartment. I pace the floor, tears in my eyes, my heart beating fast, and my stomach sinks over the thought he might have slept with someone. A knock on the door stops me.

He's quiet. "Jamie, please open the door."

"I'm tired. We can talk tomorrow."

"No, I need to see you. Please open the door."

I hesitate, listening to his voice. He's the one I trust, the one I talk to, and now should be no different. I turn the knob and he slips in, removing my hand from the knob holding on to it. He shuts the door behind him. He's now dressed in jeans and a shirt. I remove my hand from his.

"I'm not sure of much right now, but just don't shut me out."

I shake my head. "Maybe it's too late for us."

"No, don't say it." He extends his hand again.

He's my friend and has always been here for me. I can't turn away from him now. I place my hand in his. We sit on the bed together.

"Jamie what happened to you? I heard nothing for hours."

"I'm sorry. The last two days have been hard."

"What did the lawyer say?"

"A conversation for later."

He stands, walking to the dresser. "I can't explain why my room is like that or why I had no clothes on. I don't remember Stacey being here or anyone in my room."

"She made sure I knew she was here. She said the guys were playful and how she missed parties here. If you can't remember, then how can you be sure you didn't sleep with her or anyone else?"

133

His head falls forward as he realizes my words could be true. I walk over to him.

"We might not like the outcome."

He tilts my chin up, running his thumb over my cheek. He pulls me closer to him and wraps his arms around me. I don't want to pull away from him, so I move in closer.

"Jamie, I've waited a long time to tell you how much you mean to me—that I want you with me. I would never hurt you."

I look up at him. "I know that. And no matter what occurred here, I still want to be with you. You've shown me so many times who you are. You've supported, encouraged, and protected me."

He kisses the top of my head, tightening his arms around me.

"I believe in us. I'm ready to be with you."

His eyes tell me what I want to hear. He bends his head to touch my lips with his, then covers my mouth with a sweet kiss. A lingering kiss, just for us, tying us together at last. I place my hand on the back of his neck, pulling him close. When our kiss is done, we rest our heads together. Then words came from my heart.

"No more waiting or wondering. We have each other, no matter what we find out." He lowers his lips again to mine as my soul ignites with a desire I never knew existed.

*

The next morning, I sit up in bed to silence, already missing his arms around me. He stayed with me until I fell asleep but left at some point to speak to the guys still in the apartment. I take a shower, dress, and go in search of him. Looking inside his room, all linens have been removed, and the broken lamp is gone. My search finds the apartment is back to normal.

All the guys and trash have been removed. He's stretched out on the sofa and thinking he's asleep, I tiptoe to the kitchen for coffee when I hear, "Hey."

"Did I wake you?"

He sits up. "Come sit with me."

"Did you sleep at all?" He opens his arms, pulling me to his side.

"You smell good."

"Thanks, but what are your holding back?"

"Jamie, I wish I could back up time and had gone home with you. But I didn't and now I need to figure out what happened at the party."

"Does your head still hurt?"

"A little. Now who's worried?"

I want to kiss him, reassure him I'm still here for him, so I straddle his lap as he places his hands on my hips. I touch his lips with my finger, then kiss him. I like the feel of him so close to me so I move in and he matches my thought by pulling my body in as I arch into him. His hands are in my hair, tilting my head back slightly, and he kisses me so passionately my skin tingles. Then he stops abruptly.

"Let's go eat." He moves me off his lap, then stands up.

"You want to eat right now after kissing me like that. Why?"

He tries to pull me up off the sofa but I refuse, jerking my hands away. He places his hands on his hips in clear frustration. "I don't ever want to stop kissing or touching you because I've wanted to do it for so long. But because of last night, I need to stop."

"Because you slept with someone else?"

135

He turns away from me. I stand, grabbing his arm. "This affects me as well as you."

He places his hand in his back pocket, pulling out a phone, and hands it to me.

"Where did you get it?"

"In my bedroom. Let's sit down."

Fear wants me to not ask the question but I have no choice. "Whose phone?"

"Stacey's." He swipes the screen to reveal her picture. "I also found Caleb's number and intimate pictures of the two of them."

"I don't understand."

"There's more." He takes the phone, swiping it, until he finds what breaks my heart into a million pieces.

My body just forgot how to breathe so I swallow hard. "You're in bed with her, exactly how I found you. No clothes, light on in the bathroom." I toss the phone onto the sofa, then walk past him to the kitchen. I start messing with the coffee pot but his hands stop me.

"Jamie, look at me."

But I can't. It's like I had feared. My nightmare just become reality. Why is this happening?

"I would never choose to sleep with her."

"You can't remember, so maybe you did."

He hands me the phone. "Look closer at the pictures. I knew showing them to you would be hard, but I need you to look at them again. My eyes are shut in all of them. When I spoke to the other guys from that night, they had symptoms just like me. Blurry vision, headache, off balance, and they don't remember falling asleep. I think we were drugged."

I look at the pictures, seeing what he's telling me, though I'm cringing at the thought of her with him. "Why would she go to such extremes? What if someone had a reaction to whatever was given?"

"Her phone isn't locked—there's no finger, number or pattern code to open it. She wanted someone to see what she had inside."

I flip, finding several pictures of her and Caleb together. "I guess she's why he never returned my calls."

He takes hold of my hand, laying the phone on the counter. "I'm not sure what she expects to happen, unless it's to drive a wedge between us, which won't happen. You have to trust me when I say that I want to spend hours exploring every inch of you. But, until I have some answers about what happened, I can't put you at risk."

"I understand, but being intimate with you, kissing, or exploring with each other is what I've dreamed about so it ranks pretty high on my list of needs." I smile looking for a shimmer of light in his eyes.

He smiles. "I mean...we can play some."

"I like the sound of that."

*

The rest of the day he spends on the phone talking with the guys who gave him as much information as they can remember. I put away what I brought back, including the box I don't want to think about. I make some food and decide to check my emails in my room when a knock makes me look up over my computer. Michael's standing there like so many other times, but today is different.

"What are you doing?"

"Checking my assignments."

"Can I come in?"

"Yes, of course."

He lays across the bed, kissing my bare shoulder where my shirt has slid off and playing with a curl of my hair between his fingers. "I've often wondered what you did in here. I've seen you sing and dance, but what do you do when you're alone?"

I raise my eyebrow, shutting my computer and laying it on the floor beside me. Then I roll over to face him. "What do you think?"

He rolls over on his back, placing his arm under his head, and grins. "Homework, lots of reading, sleeping and dreaming of me. I died every time you walked out in yoga pants."

"Because you do or don't like yoga pants?"

"I like yoga pants on you. They really show your assets."

I push at his side and he curls slightly.

"Did you think about me in my room?"

"Yes, many times. You were probably working on your abs, playing games on the computer or doing summary sheets from work. But I hoped you were thinking of me."

"I took a lot of cold showers and didn't sleep much, knowing you were right down the hall." He turns on his side to face me. "My door is always open to you."

I lean up on my elbow. "As mine is open to you. No more apart." I touch his cheek with my fingers and hold his gaze, leaning in to kiss him but then stop. "Hungry?"

*

We hold hands walking down the sidewalk to Jimmy's Grill which has great double decker sandwiches and homemade pies. Brand new to this public show of affection on campus, I feel a sense of relief at finally being able to show him how I feel. Being this close to him makes my stomach do somersaults and warms my skin. Looking over at him, it's clear why. He captivates me, which is why waiting to be intimate with him will be hard. He stops at the door, holding it open for me. Lots of students and a few parents fill the tables, but we find a table off to the side. His fingers rub circles on my back as I can't seem to sit close enough to him.

The waitress brings our food, and all is quickly devoured, with him helping eat my sweet potato chips. He pops the last one in my mouth as he looks towards the pickup counter. "There's someone we haven't seen in a while."

I look over to find Caleb waiting for a pick-up order. He looks different to me. Thinner, wearing jeans, a blue coat, and a cap pulled down to where you can barely see his eyes. His hair was always cut short, but now it's long. He keeps looking around, kind of nervous. I know he's been with her but why? Gone is the clean-cut college student I once knew as my friend.

"Go and speak to him, I'll pay the bill."

"I want to, but then again, I don't."

"But I know you do because I can see it in your eyes."

I nod in agreement and head over to Caleb.

"Hey."

Caleb's face drains of color—at least what I can see under the growth of hair on his face. He says nothing, just looks at me.

"Are you okay? I tried all summer to reach you."

139

"Um, sorry. I need to go." He grabs his bag of food.

"Please talk to me." I touch his arm, but he jerks away. I stand there, not sure what to do.

"Jamie, are you here with anyone?" He looks around the restaurant then spots Michael coming up behind us. "I got to go."

"Caleb, we could go somewhere and talk." He turns, walking towards the door pushing through all the students. He stops turning to me. "I'm not the same guy."

"I know." He stares at me like I just told the biggest secret he didn't want me to know. This time when he speaks, he raises his voice. "Leave me alone. You don't know what I've done."

"But I do. Please call me." He stands looking at me as if he wants to do just that, talk to me. But then he turns and walks away. Michael brings me my coat.

"What did he say?"

"Nothing. He didn't want to talk to me."

"I'm sorry. Just give him some time. Maybe what you said will get him to open up."

"I hope so. Let's go home."

Chapter 21

A lot of regular runners are out this morning even with the cold temperatures. I find being outside invigorating so I guess they do as well. Now back to my therapy session. I round the corner of the Watson Building, running over the Harris Bridge that crosses the lake, thinking about last night. I slept in my bed and Michael slept in his, which is fine, but I want us together, not apart. Seeing Caleb yesterday fills my head with so many questions. How did they get together? What has he done that I don't want to know? He seems a broken shell of who I knew from before. I glance at my watch, heading back to the apartment. My playlist slows down, and I begin to walk off my run. I reach my front door to see a box addressed to Michael with his parents' return address, maybe an early Christmas gift. I take it inside, setting it on the table for later. Grabbing water and an orange, I head to my room for a shower but see a note on my nightstand.

Thinking of you! –Michael

A smile forms on my lips as I read it again. I want to call him but my phone rings before I can.

"Caleb?"

At first, he says nothing, but then his voice cracks. "Jamie, can you meet me Friday whatever time is good for you?"

"Friday night after work about 11:15—is that okay?"

"I'll meet you there. Thanks, Jamie."

Before I can say anything else, he hangs up. From our random awkward meeting yesterday to the call today, I wonder what happened. I'll text Michael later or I'm going to be late for class.

*

At the end of another academic day, which is so close to being over for winter break, I rush into 42 at 5:27, tossing my banana peel in the trash. I see Pete standing by the clock-in computer.

"Hey Jamie. How was Thanksgiving break?"

"Good and yours?"

He pats his stomach. "Delicious.. Hey, before you get your stuff, the big boss wants to see you in his office."

I start to walk away. "Thanks Pete." If he only knew how much I wanted to see my boss. I open the door to find Michael sitting behind his desk going through a stack of papers. He doesn't look up right away, giving me time to just look at him. I clear my throat.

He drops his pen, locking his eyes on me. "Hey you."

"Sometimes it's hard to believe you're a college student running a successful business. You look good in the role of boss."

"Close the door, please." He pushes away from his desk and motions for me to come over. I walk over to him and he grabs my wrist, pulling me into his lap and rests his hand on my thigh. "I caught a glimpse of you today after your second class. That was not enough."

I touch his hair, thick between my fingers. "I agree. Today is our first day back at work as an official couple."

He nuzzles my neck, leaving a few kisses. "I can't wait to let everyone know about us." He tightens his grip on me as his hand rests on my cheek, pulling me into a kiss. He breaks the magic of our kiss and asks, "Why did we wait to be this close?"

"You wanted me to be ready to accept a relationship, and I thought you were burned by your ex and wasn't ready to trust. But what we both needed was in front of us all along."

There's a knock on the door. "Michael, its Pete. We need to talk."

We look at each other. I go to stand up but I'm pulled back in his lap. "We start with Pete." He raises his voice. "Come in."

Pete opens the door holding a clipboard, sees us, and begins to smile. "So, when were you going to tell me?"

"What? That Jamie and I are a couple?"

Pete tosses the clipboard on the desk. "Finally, you spoke up and I guess Jamie, you feel the same?"

"Yes, I feel the same."

Pete walks over and I stand to face him. "Jamie you are exactly who he needs."

I smile. "It took us awhile, but we have more because of it."

Michael stands, placing his hands on my shoulders. "It's the right time."

"I saw the look on his face the day you applied for the job. There is no one else for him. You'll take care of each other because what you have is real. So, what are you waiting for? Go tell the staff."

"Pete, what did you need to talk to me about?"

"It can wait until later. I'll see you both downstairs shortly." He shuts the door and I turn, facing Michael.

143

"He seems really happy for us."

"That he is. I made a decision to meet with Stacey so I can figure out what happened at the apartment that night. I want to clear things, so we don't have to wait on anything except ourselves."

"Do you need support? She's a little crazy."

"She won't talk with you there."

"True. You know her better than me."

"I don't know this Stacey. She didn't do dumb shit like this when we were together."

"Now my turn. I'm meeting Caleb here after work on Friday. He called today after my run." I walk over to the sofa and sit down. "I know his confession will be hard to hear, but maybe he can shed some light on what she's doing."

He sits down beside me. "I don't like us having to do any of this, but we just need more answers." He threads his fingers through mine. "Are you ready to tell the staff?"

"More than ready."

When everyone's told and we close down the bar, the best part is going home together. We found out some had taken out bets on when we would actually get together, and all are happy and supportive. As we get in the apartment, I remind him of the box. I go get us water and he opens his package.

I come back to see the surprise. What is it?"

"A key."

"What kind of key?"

I look inside for another clue where I find a monogramed note card. Etched on the front in gold are the letters "LTA."

"My mother's monogram. Inside, the note reads: *Christmas awaits you in Colorado. Clear your calendar and give us a call. Love Dad & Mom.*"

"A trip! Are you surprised?"

"A little. If I go, will you go with me?"

I sip my water, dribbling out the side of my mouth. "It's for you, maybe they want to spend time with you before you graduate."

He leans in to me, holding the white ribbon attached to the key. "I go, you go."

"How can I resist? Ask them first—I don't want to cause problems just showing up."

"I can do that. Now I'm going to shower." He peels off his shirt.

We stood staring at each other, wanting to give into our feelings but remembering the agreement.

"Waiting is hard when you tease me with all your manliness."

"Manliness?"

"Yes." I run my hand across his abs, walking past him. "I have womanly ways to tempt you too though." I kick off my shoes, pull my shirt over my head, and he doesn't look away. I unbutton the top of my jeans, tugging them down a little to show my pink lace underwear. "See you after my hot shower." I turn, walking towards my room.

"Um, not playing fair using your womanly ways. Was that pink lace?

*

After my shower I chose a V neck style soft blue t-shirt to sleep in that's long enough to cover, but short enough to make him restless, just a little. My skin tingles thinking about his reaction. I open my door to find him leaning against the door frame of his room.

"I was coming to find you." He's wearing cotton workout shorts and a pullover t shirt. *How I love cotton!*

"In keeping with our deal, would you join me in my room tonight?"

"A platonic evening?"

"Yes." He holds out his hand as I walk to him. "I'm trying to stay strong but what you are wearing is not sweatpants and a hoodie."

I smile at his comment. "No, it's not."

"I know what you are doing with this little number and might I say, thank you!"

I kiss him, then walk past him into the room. *He looks so good.* He's propped up pillows and turned down his bed, with two candles lit on each side. I look back at him.

"I have popcorn, a movie, and water unless you're tired and want to just sleep."

My smile reaches ear to ear. "This is so sweet. I would love to stay with you."

We crawl in under the covers, turn on the movie, and place the popcorn between us. We talk all through the movie, stealing moments of closeness. We keep everything PG and when it ends, he blows out our candles, turns off the TV, and we lay in his bed, our arms wrapped around each other. He kisses my head.

"We'll be together soon."

"We will, but for now this is perfect."

Chapter 22

Michael

$\mathcal{I}$ lie here this morning looking at the beauty next to me. She's wearing no makeup and her hair is slightly over one eye. It would be so easy to wake her up and take our new relationship to the next level but not without knowing more about that night. I've fallen for her in a way I never thought I was capable.

Jamie

Rolling over, I reach for him, but he is gone. This is my first time waking up in a guy's bed and I miss the weight of his body next to mine. I pull the sheet up to my chin then hear the front door shut. He appears in the doorway bearing goodies.

"Good morning beautiful, how did you sleep?"

"You brought breakfast." I go to get up.

"Stay right there—it's all coming to you." He sits down on the bed. "I liked you being in here last night."

I take the coffee he hands to me. "I did too. Your mattress is so much better."

"So, you're into my mattress."

"No, I'm into you." This time I pull him to me. "I'm into these lips and these arms that held me all night." He takes my coffee cup and tosses the sandwiches on the table, scooting me down in the bed and wrapping me up in everything Michael.

*

Friday night at work proved to be busy but finally we were standing at the end of the bar waiting for Caleb.

"Why don't you cancel with him or let me tag along?"

"I'm not cancelling and he might say something to me about the party if you're not there."

He pulls me up against him and I giggle when he starts nibbling my neck. "I like that way too much."

"What this?"

I'm enjoying his lips brushing up against my neck when he suddenly stops. "He's here."

Caleb comes in dressed like I saw him that night.

"I don't like this."

I squeeze Michael's hand. "I'm aware, but I need to do it."

I turn to Caleb. "Hi."

Michael sticks out his hand. "Nice to see you again."

Caleb holds out his hand to acknowledge the greeting. "Good to see you. Jamie, is Dot's okay with you?"

"Yes." I turn to Michael. "See you later."

Caleb turns walking to the door and I follow but turn back and wink at Michael who is standing with his arms crossed, looking at us. Always protective.

*

Our walk to Dot's was quiet with a few glances and basic questions about school or the weather. We found a table, then placed an order for coffee. I took off my coat and then he took off his cap.

"Wow, your hair is so long."

He seems to be self-conscious about my comment because he places the cap on backwards. The waitress sets down our coffee mugs.

"Caleb, are you alright, are you sick?"

He rests his elbows on the table, looking down into his coffee. "No. I'm not sick. I'm ashamed to be here with you."

I sit back in my chair. "What? Ashamed to be seen with me? Why did you call me if you didn't want to be seen with me?"

"No, that's not what I meant."

"Well jump in, because I'm about to leave."

He is struggling to even look at me.

"Just tell me what happened to you. We were friends, then you disappeared."

"Do you remember last year after the 42 party when we went into your apartment?"

"Yes. I remember telling you I was a virgin, we ate sandwiches and watched a movie. Caleb, what does that have to do with you not returning my calls?"

"I liked you. I enjoyed being with you. I wanted more with you, but I understood what you said about waiting and not being ready. But after that, as the weeks passed, my feelings grew stronger—yours did not."

"Caleb."

"The only way to put you out of my mind was to put distance between us, maybe find someone else. I started drinking and attending every party I could. One night at a party in BETA House I was so wasted and a redheaded girl sat down next to me. She was also drunk but it led us into making out there, then going back to her place. I woke up the next morning alone in a girl's bed with a massive headache. I went looking for her and ibuprofen only to find her in the kitchen in my shirt and long blonde hair. When she turned to face me, it was Stacey."

"You knew what she did to Michael and how she was with me just for living in the apartment with him. You also knew what she looked like."

"She wore a wig and dressed like an average college student. Everything I knew about her disappeared because of how she made me feel. I began to spend more time with her which made it easier not being with you. I know that sounds shitty, but I knew deep down that Michael was into you and what I saw of you two together, you were falling for him."

"You just stopped talking to me. I don't throw relationships aside for others. We could have been supportive of each other whether we were together or not."

"I know that now, but the road I took was not one I wanted you to be on. I drank, even took some pills that kept me in a state of not being able to do any part of my life, except being with her at her apartment. I left my family, school, and you. I am sorry."

"Do you still want to be with her?"

"Now that my head is clear, thanks to a letter from my sister and seeing you the other night, it makes me want something different for myself. I want to get back into school, stop the drinking, and hope my family and friends will take me back."

"It all sounds good."

"Well it won't be easy knowing the kind of hurt I left along the way. She lied to me. I think she has a plan to get Michael back and used my connection with you."

"How?"

"She wanted me to talk about you, where you were from, who your friends were, etc. She wants you away from him. I think she did something the night of the party at your apartment."

"Like what?"

"She spoke with someone on the phone and knew you were out of town."

"But how would she know that? Do you know what she did?"

"No, I passed out on the bed before she left. But the next day she was all over me, happy, and assured me things would be different soon for the both of us. I don't know what that meant." He folds his hands in front of him. "You may never forgive me, but I'm done with her for good. I never meant harm to either of you, but I know in giving her certain information, it might come back to cause issues for you both."

I look into my mug, then back at him. "I don't trust her because of what happened that night and I'm glad you are away from her." We both stand as I put on my coat. "I usually like people or find something in them I like, but not Stacey. She seems to go the extra mile to hurt people."

"I see that now that my mind is clear."

"Caleb, it's not up to me or anyone else to say who you can be with, but I'm glad you realized who she really is. You will find yourself again, just give it time."

"Thanks for meeting with me. I am trying to make everything right again."

*

When I arrive home, I feel confused. Knowing he was with her, telling her things about me, and that she still wants Michael frustrates me. He let go of himself for so many months, and the fact that he was used by her to help in whatever plan she has makes me sick. I wipe tears off my face and see Michael on the sofa watching a game.

"Hey, who's playing?"

He turns around. "Are you okay?"

I sit beside him on the sofa.

"How did it go?"

"He's so different—not only in appearance, but he told me he was drinking, even taking pills that kept him in a fog. He not only stopped talking with me but he cut off contact with his family. I hope he can find his way back because I miss the Caleb I knew before.

*

We both wake up to a blank blue screen a few hours later, cozy on the sofa.

I pull out my hair tie. "Um, it's late."

"Are you feeling better?"

153

"With you, yes."

"Want to talk about Caleb?"

"You saw him that night at the restaurant. He let so much of himself go to be with her."

"But why Stacey?"

"He said he liked me and wanted to take our relationship to the next step, but I didn't. To get me off his mind he started drinking and going to parties. They met at a fraternity party and she was wearing a red wig. Both of them were drunk and he went home with her. He said she helped him not think of me, so he drank, popped pills and didn't see his family. He did talk about the night of the party but just that she spoke with someone on the phone, then when she came back home that night she was happy."

"I get the trying to be numb to forget something—I've done that. Caleb threw away what was real for him by turning to her. Did he leave her for good?"

"He said he did. He wants to be better, be himself again."

"Good."

"He is pretty sure she wants you back or at least wants me gone. He told her things about me, my family and friends back home."

"Why?"

"I don't know."

He smiles, pulling me up off the sofa. "She is jealous because I lost my heart to you because of the goodness I see in your eyes and the huge heart that you have open to everyone. What I had with Stacey was drama, bad behavior, and self-destruction. What you give me is nothing that she is capable of giving to another person."

154

"Well I hope this light he has seen continues because I see nothing good for him being with her."

"How about we go to bed and maybe go to brunch at Dot's tomorrow?"

Like any girl who lives for food and the company of a great guy, I agree to his proposition immediately. "Sounds good."

*

Michael

As I tuck Jamie into my left arm with her head resting on my chest, we go to bed no closer to solving our dilemma, but I know I want Stacey out of our lives for good. I even want her away from Caleb. Crazy does not cover what she has done but knowing how far she will go to get the results she wants disturbs me. The next morning Jamie has research to do with her study group in the library this morning, so we decide no brunch and I grab a quick cup of coffee before heading to the bar. I hand the barista my card when painted red nails slide around my waist resting on my shirt.

"Hey, handsome."

I jerk around. "Stacey, what the hell are you doing?"

"Come on, don't you remember the last time I touched you and how much you liked it?"

The girl on the other side of the counter cuts her eyes at me. I grab Stacey by the arm and pull her towards the hall towards the bathrooms, hoping not to let anyone else hear her. She yanks her arm away, rubbing her elbow.

"I like to play rough too, sometimes," she says, smiling coyly at me.

"What are you doing?"

"What do you mean?"

"Let's start with the party."

"You want to talk about what you did to me or what I lovingly did to you?"

"Why were you there?" She steps towards me as I step back away from her.

"Why are you so cold to me after what we rediscovered?"

"Are you taking some type of delusional drug? Because I would never choose to be with you."

"We have heat you and I—she can't give you that."

It takes everything I have to stay calm. I've never hit a woman, but she could be the first. "I know you drugged a few of us the night of the party. What I want to know is why you gave it to us and what you were trying to accomplish with the fake pictures."

"Nothing fake. There was a lot of alcohol in the apartment. I think you forgot how to have fun."

I turn, running my hands through my hair in frustration. "Stop with the lies. What are you doing with Caleb? You made it clear by not locking your phone you wanted us to see all your pictures."

She begins to smile. "He was in need of companionship and I needed the distraction."

"You have no idea how you hurt people. You need counseling. Stay away from me, away from Jamie, and leave Caleb the hell alone. I'm tired of this bullshit you've fabricated."

I turn to leave when she grabs my coat. "Don't leave. Let's talk some more."

My body stiffens. "Let go."

She waves her hands in surrender. "We're meant to be together, you'll see."

I pull out my phone and call Jamie leaving the coffee shop. Stacey has clearly snapped transforming into someone I don't recognize at all. *Come on Jamie, pick up. I need to hear your voice.* She answers quietly.

"Hey, handsome, miss me already?"

"Where are you?"

"I'm in the library. Is something wrong?"

"I'm coming to you, please wait for me."

*

Jamie

I slip my phone in my back pocket. Something is wrong, but what? I look up to see him suddenly in front of me, but unsmiling and clearly upset. He reaches for my hand, saying nothing as I follow behind him to an aisle in the back of the library. He backs me up against the shelf of books which is a hot move, but something is wrong. His fingers trace along the inside of my hands that he's holding close to my sides. He's trying to calm down before speaking so I wait. He takes one of my hands, placing it over his heart.

"Jamie, this is where you are, where you've always been. I like who I am with you. I don't want to wait any longer to be with you if you still want me."

My other hand touches his cheek, feeling the prick of his stubble from not shaving this morning. "I don't want to wait either. Tell me what happened."

"I just left the Coffee Hut where Stacey magically appeared. She acts like we're a couple. I told her I felt all of it was staged the night of the party and that she drugged me and a few of the other guys."

"She denied it, I'm sure."

"We'll never get the truth about that evening."

"No, we won't." His eyes are different now. All the anger and frustration from earlier now gone replaced by gentle caring eyes who want me.

"I trust your beautiful green eyes with my life. Are you ready for the next step in our commitment to one another?"

Touching his cheek I nod my head yes. "I'm ready for whatever comes our way."

We kiss without holding back. Our connection to one another started months ago and now we can finally give in to the feelings we have for each other.

Chapter 23

After taking a difficult exam and turning in another paper, I'm looking forward to having dinner with Michael. After the encounter with Stacey, he is more than ready to move on and so am I. We are ready for what is to come, taking each step for us. Arriving at the apartment with little time to get ready, I choose an outfit I hope drives him crazy wanting me. Black heels and a green dress that grabs my curves, I smooth out the material and look in the mirror, tucking a small portion of hair behind my right ear. I head down the hall to his room, where I'm stopped in my tracks at the sight of him. It's not just the tailored blue suit he's wearing that fits him perfectly, but the look in his eyes as he sees me. Yep, that's what I want.

"You look handsome."

He walks towards me. "I'm trying to make a good impression on someone special."

"Totally impressed. Where are we eating?"

"Angelo's."

"Yum, let me gab my coat."

He grabs my hand, turning me to face him. "Not before I tell you how beautiful you are right now."

"Well, I'm also trying to impress someone very special."

"Definitely did that and more."

We arrive at the restaurant which has a long line out front, but he keeps walking to the hostess stand. Angelo's is a high-end establishment in town, serving authentic Italian food from recipes handed down in the family. Not a lot of college kids but it stays packed.

He steps up. "Reservation Tucker."

The hostess gives menus to another woman. "Lane will seat you. Enjoy your evening."

Okay, she's eyeing him like he's an appetizer up for grabs. I link my arm into his, *Yes, all mine, menu closed.* I smile, thinking *petty but great.*

All the tables are covered in white tablecloths with white dishes trimmed in blue, but on our table, there is a vase of pink peonies.

I look around at the other tables. "Did you do this?"

"Yes, because I know you love them."

"So sweet. Thank you." He helps me out of my coat then holds the chair for me. I sit, but not before grabbing one of the flowers, holding it to my nose.

"They remind me of your first night in the apartment. You came out hair wet, fresh from a shower, smelling like this flower."

"That night I spilled out my life to you and hoped you were not going to regret me taking the room."

"If you hadn't said yes, I would have pleaded with you." He reaches over, touching my hand with his fingers. "I was instantly intrigued by a girl from Texas and needed to know more about her."

Our waitress brings drinks, a basket of various breads, and we place our orders. It's then that he asks the question I've been putting aside.

"You haven't said much about your trip home. What happened?"

I twist my bread into small pieces as it becomes real again. "I have a sister."

He stops drinking water and sets the glass down with a confused look. "What?"

"Where do I start? My dad wrote a letter to me a while back in case he died before he could tell me. He admits to a tryst with a woman who lived in a town near where my parents lived. The woman was also married. A few months later, she broke the news that she was pregnant with his baby. She wanted to stay with her husband, raise the child as his, and have my dad relinquish all rights. But if he persisted, she would destroy his life, his marriage, and he would never see the baby. He went home to tell my mom but that afternoon at a doctor's appointment, she was told her cancer was back. He didn't tell her after all. After treatments for her illness, she became pregnant with her miracle baby, me." I sit back in my chair out of breath.

"Jamie, why didn't you tell me sooner?"

"Things have been a little crazy since my return. But there's more. The point of him paying tuition at Hopson, so far away from my home, is that he found out a couple years ago that she's a student here or went here at one point. He thought by putting me in or near her I would have family and not be alone."

"Did Ruby know?"

"Yes, but as I told her, it was not her place to tell me, so I don't blame her. I'm not sure how I feel about it. Do I find her or just let it go?"

The waitress sets down our food, which looks delicious. We thank her, then I look at Michael who is staring at me, not the culinary masterpiece in front of him.

"I can't tell you how to feel about what you learned, but I'm here if you need help or just want to talk."

"Thank you. Look at me—I broke the rule of talking about issues other than us tonight."

He gets up and walks over to me, leaning down so our faces are even. "We are a team. If we need to talk about anything, we talk. I want to be in your life, not running on the outside." He touches my face, kissing me. "Ready to eat?"

"Yes."

*

Our dinner was truly an authentic fantasy trip to Italy. I'm beginning to feel nervous about what might happen when we get home. Not scared or regretful, but nervous if I'll do the right thing or be the person he has been thinking about for months. Once we get home, I set my purse down and take off my coat, laying it across the sofa turning to him.

"Thank you for a delicious meal."

"I enjoyed mine and a little of yours. But something is bothering you, what is it?"

"I… I'm nervous—are you nervous? You probably are not. What am I saying? You have been with girls intimately before, so I'm sure you are not nervous."

He raises his hands up and cups my face. "But I am."

"Help me understand that."

"You woke up my heart, my way of thinking, and restored my trust. I have feelings about you that have never surfaced with anyone else. You know my past with girls, but not a single one made me feel like you do. I don't want to mess this up either. What if *I'm* not what you want?"

I kiss him.

"I am thankful every day for you and who you are." My hands rest on his chest where I play with the buttons on his shirt. "May I?"

He stands, letting me take my time. One button, then another, as I lay kisses on his bare chest, touching his skin with my fingers. He takes in a breath. I pull his shirt out of his pants, then he helps to take it off, laying it on the sofa. I've seen him shirtless many times before but tonight he is all mine to touch and explore. He has physical strength clearly, but he's opening his heart to me and I want to protect him. He lets out a moan. I smile to myself, knowing I did that.

"May I unzip your dress?"

I turn, facing away from him and pull my hair to the side. He trails kisses all the way down my neck onto my shoulder while pulling at the zipper, holding the dress as I step out. I turn to face him, his eyes make me blush and I feel it all over. I wore a black lace bra with matching lace undies.

He picks me up, wrapping my legs around his waist as I let out a small sound. He walks to his room with me in his arms-- a hot move I've read about in books, but now it's happening to me. I lay on my back with him propped on his elbow, running his fingers across the thin fabric.

"I am going to enjoy unwrapping every layer."

He takes his time removing each shoe or article of clothing, leaving a trail of kisses on my skin. My breathing is faster and my body is moving, aching for him. He stands up to remove the rest of his clothes and I roll over onto my stomach so I can admire him. He lowers himself onto the bed, but not before kissing the small of my back up to my shoulder. I move my arms to turn and face him as his mouth lowers to mine. He stops.

"You might feel some discomfort—tell me if you need me to stop."

"I will."

He moves over me, bending his arms next to me with his hands right above my head. He knows what he wants and my body is in agreement. I have a strong feeling of wanting to connect with him, not realizing I'm holding my breath.

"Jamie, breathe."

At that moment his eyes lock with mine, his voice soothes me, and my hands go into his hair, pulling him down to kiss him. "I want you."

He pushes as I let out a small noise, watching him watching me. "Okay?"

"Yes." From that point on, our bodies take over, leading us to pleasures that were a long time coming.

*

We lay in his bed, our limbs tangled up as I trace circles on his stomach. He nuzzles against my hair, as I make more circles on his chest. He grabs my hand, placing it against his.

"Your hands are petite next to mine."

"Yes they are, so I fit inside yours perfectly." I wrap mine around his, bringing it to my lips kissing his knuckles. "You know as a girl I had thoughts about my first experience with a guy, but I didn't know my body would react that way—which leaves me curious about other things."

He flips me over where he's above me smiling. "Is there anything you want to try right now? I am more than happy to nurture a healthy curiosity."

Chapter 24

We spend the next few days exploring my curiosities, especially one in the shower that will stay in my memory bank for a long time. In fact, thinking of that got me in trouble with my professor who wanted to know what was more important than his class. Not able to give him one out loud he volunteered me to return video equipment to the library, so I could get a breath of fresh air which I did gladly. Michael has taken me to a place of no return which suits me fine. The one thing I am not looking forward to is the HCSW meeting tomorrow. I decided to withdraw my membership but I needed to do it in person. Her personal agenda and actions of late prove to me I can't be around her. Maybe next year when she is gone I will reconsider.

*

I slam the door to HCSW behind me. UGH! The most ridiculously one-sided meeting I've ever attended. Why does Stacey or any of the senior board members think they can get away with all the changes without writing them up, presenting them, and having a vote? No warning, no discussion. Heck, over half of the new girls will leave and the work won't get done. All those families, the tutoring program, all for what? Dressing a certain way, paying outlandish dues? That's not going to fly. I rub at my arm where her nails dug in to keep me from leaving. I walk briskly, shaking my head and trying to purge what just happened. That altercation with her was my last and now I am done. I check my watch for the time when I hear my name.

"Jamie wait, stop walking." Ashley is coming towards me fast and out of breath. "Clearly I need more physical activity. Did she threaten you?"

"You heard all that?"

"Yes. What the hell is wrong with her?"

"I'm dating her ex so *that* drama is nothing new."

"History or not, that was wrong. You might want to call campus security."

"I put up with so much—as of today I'm done. I hope others figure out who she is before investing too much."

"Look, as a new member I don't know either of you well but when she grabbed your arm and said those words, well, that girl is crazy."

I giggle at her facial expression. "Well, thank you for saying that. I liked the work they were able to do when I joined last year, but now there is no way I can stay."

"Oh, after what I encountered, I'm out too."

"Good decision. Hopefully others will pull away or make her leave. I need to get to work. See you soon."

*

When I arrive at 42 I'm less agitated, but still frustrated by what she did. I head to the back and clock in, then grab my bucket and begin bussing tables, filling water pitchers, and soda orders. I load the washing machine with towels, then put the dishes into the washer. I step back, take a breath, and put my hair back up. As my fingers fumble with the tie, arms wrap around my waist.

"I've had an image of your hair falling down your bare back all day."

I turn to face him. "Have you now? Well I have the memory of a particular shower that lingered over into class, which got me in trouble with Professor Yates."

"Thoughts of me over philosophy, I like it." He kisses me. "I saw you come in but with the flu and electronic issues I couldn't properly say hello."

"Pete texted that three people are out, and no one has heard from Leslie."

"I finally did, and she has strep. Do you need help on the floor? I could free up a bartender?"

"No, they make you money and I can do this alone for now. I have a lot of energy."

"How was your meeting?"

I'm still fuming on the inside but it's not a conversation to have now when we're so busy. "We can talk at dinner." I place my arms around his middle, just needing the weight of his hug.

"Come on guys, the two of you make me very happy, but we are dying out there." I walk past Pete and smile. "Thank you, Jamie."

"You're welcome."

"Man, I need you behind the bar because two taps aren't working properly and I'm going upstairs for change."

"Okay, I'm on it. Crazy tonight huh?"

*

The evening progresses without incident even though we're short on employees. I take a moment to drink some water when I feel a tap on my shoulder. It's Caleb, sitting at the table next to me with two other guys. I've seen him twice since our talk, but we text regularly. I want to help so Michael and I both agreed being there for him is what he needs.

"Hey, Jamie."

"You made it."

"These guys arrived about an hour ago. This place is packed. What's the specials tonight?"

"BBQ and hand cut chips and two-for-one wings."

"This is Oron and Rob—my friends from high school I told you about."

They stood reaching for my hand. "Nice to meet you both. Welcome to 42! Um, Jenny is your waitress but she's over there, so let me take your order."

I drop the order at the back window along with my bucket in the kitchen, then head to the bar. All the bartenders, including Michael, are slammed. I look over at Caleb and he does seem better. He cut his hair, started going to the gym, hasn't had alcohol or drugs, and is back in school full swing. His parents encouraged him to see a counselor which he does Tuesday and Thursday nights. I head back to their table with drinks after letting Jenny know what I did. She gives me a hug for helping her out.

"Here are your drinks, food will be out soon, and I have tokens for all of you. Go crazy! We have new video games in the back room, enjoy!"

I return to the kitchen when an order bell dings. "Delivery to table five—Jamie, can you do it?"

"I got it." I head to table five, when I notice a small group of girls come in and sit down at a table I have yet to clean off but was going to get next. What I hear then is a nails-on-the-chalkboard kind of voice.

"Excuse me, excuse me. Can we get our table cleaned off? Or maybe I should wave down the owner. He should know about his inept workers."

Oh no you don't. With a smile on my face, I turn to find Stacey with three girls, one of whom I remember from the night of the party outside my apartment.

"I can clean it for you."

"Oh, Jamie. I never realized it, but this job fits you perfectly. Cleaning up trash, washing dishes—I guess you aren't old enough yet to be a real waitress." The girls are snickering at her comments.

Every muscle in my body stiffens. *Breathe, be the bigger person.* They all back away from the table as I remove the bottles and sanitize. When I'm all loaded up, I go to walk away.

"You missed a spot."

I see nothing but wipe it once more.

"Look, ladies, there he is—Michael Tucker, captain of Hopson's rowing team."

"He's cute—why did you walk away from him?"

"What I wouldn't do to run my fingers through his hair and feel those whiskers brush against my skin." She made a motion across her chest. She leans on the table with her elbows. "He has many hidden talents."

Do they really believe her? I need to leave before this escalates. When I turn away from the table, I feel a push against my back. The bottles on the tray shift and in a few horrible seconds it goes crashing to the floor. A

169

loud crash to me, but because of the music no one really noticed. I'm mortified and immediately bend down to clean it up. When I finish, I look over at her table where I see them whispering. She did this to me. I walk closer to them.

"You pushed me—what is wrong with you?"

"Why would I do that? I am a customer waiting patiently to be serviced." She looks past me and spots Caleb. "I guess you're inadequate with a tray as you were with him." She gets out of the booth, making her way to me. The only thing separating us is my tray. "Just like I said earlier, pathetic."

I go to walk away without another word but stop. "Why are you here, again?"

"I'm here for him. He'll know soon enough why he needs me."

"You're a sad delusional person if you think he'll ever take you back."

"I know him better than you think. He's a guy who needs to let loose, take a walk on the wild side. You're plain, simple, and uninteresting."

"Michael was right when he said you were crazy and even that word is not strong enough to cover your insanity." I turn to walk away but find myself heading face first towards the floor with the tray and all its contents, again. It takes me a moment to shake off yet another embarrassment, but I come back up to face her. "You tripped me."

"No! Girls, did you see anything?" She reaches out and pushes my shoulder. I try to hold back, but it's too late. I push her backwards with both hands and in retaliation, she comes at me this time pushing me into a table of customers.

"That's it!" Everything I have bottled up inside of me explodes and I push her so hard, her tall frame in her expensive shoes fall against a chair. I hear a noise coming from her that sounds like a crazed animal and she reaches for me with both hands. I find my inner fighter and for however long we're two girls locked in a hair pulling, kicking and screaming match. When we break away from each other, I fall back on the floor and she stumbles and catches herself on a table. I stand up, moving my hair from my face as she paces back and forth.

"You'll never have him, Jamie. He's my future, not yours."

"Stacey, this is over. Michael is with me. You need to accept it and move on."

Just like that, she walks forwards and slaps me across the face hard enough to jerk my head to the side. I pull back my fist to hit her, but someone grabs me around my waist. I turn to see Caleb holding me in place.

"She smacked me in the face." I turn back to her and she does it again. My face is now on fire. "Caleb, let me go! I'm not done with her."

This time he yells at her. "Stacey, stop! This is not what you need to do."

She looks at him almost like what he said registered with her. They're locked onto each other. The crowd thickens, keeping us in a private circle.

I struggle against his arm breaking the silence. "Caleb, let me go." He tightens his grip.

"Jamie, she will use this against you because she's incapable of backing off."

She steps up close to us. I wait for her to say something but instead she draws her hand up to hit me again, until her hand is caught by someone. She whips around to face Michael.

"This ends now." He looks at me. "Okay?" I nod. He turns his attention back to her. "You are not allowed back in the 42. You went too far this time."

She tries pulling away from him, but he tightens his grip on her wrist, pulling her away from us.

"Jamie started it. I was only trying to protect myself, protect you."

"Me? What the hell for? You protect no one but yourself. You are incapable of caring or being rational."

"You have to hear me out."

"NO!" He pulls her towards the door as her friends follow. She goes to reach for him but the bouncer is now helping to assist her departure as all three head outside.

*

Outside the bar...

"Michael, you're not listening to me. She started all of this. Why are you listening to her poison?"

"Enough! Not another word about Jamie. You need to listen to yourself and remember why we broke up. We were done long before I caught you sleeping with my best friend. You pushed me to do things that were

destroying me, so you could show everyone you saved me. I was stupid to let you do it as long as you did. Stop making a fool of yourself and get on with your life. I will file papers tomorrow so you can't come back."

"You and I are tied together, you'll see." Blowing me a kiss she leaves with her friends.

Pete had walked out and is now next to me, so I ask him. "What the hell is wrong with her?"

"What does she mean that you both are tied together?"

I turn to go back inside. "Not sure."

"Michael, if she's not concerned about doing this to Jamie in public, what will she do if they're ever alone?"

That thought hits me hard. "I need to go check on Jamie."

"Go. I'll wait to be sure she's gone."

Back inside the bar

"Caleb, you can let go of me."

"Are you sure?"

"Yes, I'm sure." I go about picking up everything off the floor and he bends to help.

We start back to the kitchen when a few people cheer for me. One girl said Stacey needed the beat down, but I'm devastated I let her get to me.

Caleb sets the tray on the counter. "Jamie, you can't let down your guard. She seemed desperate to do this in here. She had to know he would be on your side." He touches my face. "Does it hurt?"

I see Michael standing in the doorway. Caleb looks at him. "I'm going to leave so you two can talk."

"Thanks for your help," I say.

"I'm sorry it went that far."

Michael slaps Caleb on the shoulder. "Thanks for your help back there."

Caleb smiled. "I'm glad I was there." I watch him leave, turning my attention to the one walking towards me. He places a finger on my chin, tilting it to see my cheek better. "How you doing, slugger?"

"I'm so sorry." He walks to the first aid kit on the wall and activates a cold pack. "Here, put this on your cheek and tell me why you're sorry."

"I shouldn't have reacted the way I did. I'm sorry it was here, it's so embarrassing."

"Look, we both know she needed an ass kicking." I giggle, grabbing my face. "She probably didn't think you would fight back."

"It's unnerving to me what she said."

He pulls me to him, locking his arms around me, and kissing the top of my head. "She's not allowed back here. I will file papers in the morning."

"We had words earlier and I quit the club."

"Do you think that's what sparked the fight?"

"She said some threatening words, grabbed my arm, and some of the other girls saw it."

"I'm sorry you have to be a part of this. How about we get you some soup or a steak for your cheek."

I poked him in his chest. "Real cute, mister."

"Come on my little spitfire—I have to write a report on the incident."

"Serious?"

"I'm afraid so."

*

After my altercation with Stacey, coming home to a long hot shower is exactly what I needed. We crawl into bed and my body collapses against his. The weight of his arm across my hip lets me relax and I fall asleep quickly. I wake up sometime later from a nasty dream that Stacey hit me but realize from my tender cheek it was real. I go seek out ice and a small snack. I fill a freezer bag with ice and spread slices of bread with almond butter and strawberry jam. After the first bite, I decide on a tall glass of milk. Three bites in, Michael appears rubbing his eyes.

"Did I wake you?"

"No, I woke up and you were gone. How is the chewing and your cheek?"

"Okay. Would you like a sandwich?"

He pulls up a stool next to me. "Sure."

I deliver him his sandwich and he pulls me in between his legs. He eats his in about four bites. "Good choice."

"I'm glad you like it."

"You know the Colorado trip is coming up. I called my parents and it will just be you and me."

"In that case, I would love to go with you."

175

He places a kiss on my shoulder. "Great. I'll book the flight tomorrow but right now, you need to get your cute butt back to bed."

He picks me up, placing me on his shoulder, and takes me to bed for the second time that night.

Chapter 25

Our trip to Colorado is really happening and my bags were packed two days before our departure day. Our first trip as a couple is going to be in cold weather, but I packed a few small treasures I think he will like to warm things up. We spend the airplane ride with him telling me about where we're staying, along with a little history about the area. His parents took care of all the arrangements, his mom showing excitement over the phone that I could go with him. Arriving at the cabin, I'm taken back by the size of it, plus our view of the snow covered mountains. Michael visited often as a child which gives him a huge advantage on skiing as I have never been on a real course before. The door opens to an impressive looking room with overstuffed furniture and thick rugs covering the hardwood floors. The kitchen was next, with stainless steel appliances and an island separating the space from the living room. I open the fridge, never having seen one so big in a residence before and I find platters of fruits, veggies and meats along with containers of prepared foods.

"Who did this?"

"My mother. She wants us to relax and enjoy ourselves not to worry about cooking. In fact, she took care of most everything for the trip."

"We'll have to thank her with a nice gift."

I make my way down the hall to a huge bedroom with a beautiful four poster bed. The attached bathroom had big fluffy white towels and an abundance of toiletries. Michael watches me from the doorway, leaning against the frame.

"I've never seen anything like this." I go to the window in the bedroom and look out over snow covered trees. "Is this where you spent your time growing up?"

"Not this particular cabin." He comes to the window. "We stayed in Maddox—the next county over. Maybe 15 minutes from here. Now what do you want to do first?"

I look up at him smiling. "Ski."

*

We agree on skiing while there is still light. I need gear and an instructor and I talk him into skiing on the mountain of his choice while I learn to use the skis properly. We set a time to meet for a late lunch at the café.

My instructor Brian was thorough, giving me the skills to tackle a beginner's slope and maybe even an intermediate. My running clearly paid off—my legs are stronger and my stamina takes me through the next 2 ½ hours of skiing fun. I check my phone, noticing it's time to meet Michael, so I return to the lodge, handing in my gear and begin to walk over to meet him.

I find it odd that snow is on the ground, the sun is out, and I'm sitting outside enjoying a cup of hot tea not freezing. Minutes later I spot him walking towards me with two other guys. He comes over to the table and kisses me.

"Hey gorgeous, how was your lesson?"

"Pretty good. I have a few skills to take to the slopes now."

One of the guys clears his throat. "We're still here."

"Sorry guys." Michael turns back to them. "Jamie, I want to introduce you to Max and Parker. My friends from high school."

Extending my hand. Max meets me first. "Tell me, why are you with him? Michael, she is too pretty for you." Parker takes my hand, kissing it and moving in front of Michael.

"Nice to meet you."

Max grabs Parker by the arm and shoulder. "Come on Don Juan. The party is at 8:00. You two come by for a little while so we can catch up."

Michael reaches out, shaking their hands. "Good to see you both." Once they leave, he takes a seat at the table.

"What party?"

"There's a party tonight at Max's cabin."

"Friends since high school—how can you say no? Maybe I can hear some stories about you back in the day."

"I just hope you'll want to be with me after you hear those stories."

"Nothing could change how I feel about you."

He touches my cheek. "I like to hear that."

We eat our sandwiches, then spend a few hours exploring the resort. After a while, we decide to walk back to our cabin, enjoying handmade caramels.

*

Now inside the cabin Michael stands watching me while I peel off my layers of clothing.

"What are you thinking?"

"I'm amazed how you calm and excite me all at the same time. What magic do you have over me?"

I pull the tie from my hair, shaking it loose, and bend over and unzip my boot, slipping it off, then the next one. I pull my long sleeve shirt off over my head and then take off my pants, stripping down to my sports bra and underwear.

"No magic." I walk to him. "We opened ourselves up to explore our feelings." I start pulling off his shirt. "There is trust between us." I unsnap his pants. "You would do anything to make me happy and I would do the same for you."

"You're right." He kisses me. "We have time before the party want to get in the hot tub?"

"That will make us both happy."

He shows me how the knobs work, then he leaves coming back with two bottles of water lowering himself into the tub. I scoot next to him.

"Tell me about the friends we'll see tonight."

"Max has been around the longest, which means he's seen all of my antics growing up. He played a part in some, but the ones with my dad—he was there to pick up the pieces. Parker I met in tenth grade and he's still speaking to me. I realize now I was a brat and an ass."

"If you were, you are not now. I'll enjoy meeting anyone who knew you back then. I've never heard their names before today. How come?"

"Max travels a lot and Parker is actually based in Europe. We touch base when I'm at home sometimes if they are in town. Now how about a shower?"

"Sounds perfect."

*

I sit in front of the vanity wrapped in a towel. He is in the huge closet where we placed our bags. "Michael what do we wear tonight?"

He comes into the bedroom, wearing nothing but a towel, and holds up his hands. "What about this?"

"No, that you wear only for me."

"Aww, possessive of her man, I like that. Then I will go and find something else, clothes that please the lady. Can I bring you something from the closet?"

"Sure." I wait patiently to see what he will bring out. A few minutes later, he appears in a pair of blue jeans, holding a pair of black skinny jeans and a red pullover shirt for me.

"How about these?"

"They are nice, but is this all?

He smiles a devilish smile. "I did find these." He holds up a white set of lingerie that have tiny red dots all over the lace material. "I picked these for me."

When I finish dressing and fussing with my hair, I head out to the kitchen. He whistles.

"Thank you, sir."

He hands me a glass of red wine which I sniff. *Hmm.* I turn it up, draining the glass, and set it on the counter.

"Too fast?"

He laughs. "Not at all. Are you nervous?"

"That obvious, huh?"

He takes my hands and pulls me over to his side. "I should be the one nervous about what you might hear tonight."

"I will love stories about you. One more small glass?"

He pours me half of what I had before. I turn it up, draining it.

"Okay now I'm ready."

*

We arrive at a tucked away two-story house at the end of a dirt road. It's well lit, and has large windows all across the front, where people are coming and going from the house. We make our way past the people on the porch and I'm amazed by the exposed beams, furniture, and the art on the wall. There's a huge fireplace in the middle of the room. I'm just looking around at everything when I hear Max. He heads towards us, loudly calling out Michael's name which sends eyes and attention in our direction. He matches Michael in height with a short buzz cut and sports a blue sweater and khaki pants. He looks past Michael at me and I smile.

"Hey Max."

He leans in, grabbing my hand and planting a kiss on my cheek. "You are too pretty for this Neanderthal."

"That she is. Max, where's Maci?"

"Talking somewhere, being a lovely hostess. You guys mingle, get a drink, and leave your coats over to the right. Don't think you're splitting early because there's a lot of booze and good times to be had."

We drop off our coats and get a glass of wine when we hear a woman's voice call out Michael's name. A tall, leggy blonde is coming our direction and fast. She's wearing jeans, a strapless white top, and black suede booties that give her even more height. She wraps her long arms around Michael's neck and kisses him.

"Max told me he saw you today. We've missed you and I am so glad you came tonight. We have so much to catch up on."

"Maci, this is my girlfriend, Jamie Morgan."

Maci moves in front of me.

"Where are my manners? Max told me about you." She reaches out, grabbing me. "I have juicy information about your man, but first— do you like wine spritzers? I want to know all about you and the powers you used to catch the heart of this one. Michael, I'm going to steal this little cutie for a while."

She takes me by the hand and starts to lead me away, but not before tapping Max on the chest as we walk by him. "You boys go and get caught up, Jamie will be fine with me."

*

I watch my girlfriend being led away then I'm smacked on my back by Max. "She's in good hands. Let's go check out the bar in the other room with the private reserve."

"I see Maci hasn't changed."

"No, she is bossy, opinionated, and still gets my blood pumping. I need therapy clearly."

I walk behind Max into a smaller room no one else is allowed in and see a large rock fireplace and an all wood bar. "Now this is impressive."

"Pull up a stool." Max pulls out a glass bottle and two tumblers, filling them halfway.

183

I turn it up. "How long have your parents owned this house? Because I don't remember all of this."

"Since I was seven or eight. They want to give it to us."

"Really?"

Max props himself up on the bar with his elbows. "Yes, but the catch is that we have to be married for the title switch."

"Well the two of you have been together a long time, what are you waiting for?"

"She's the one who wants to wait. Besides I'm in no hurry either. What about you? The girl out there isn't the typical girl you usually go for."

"What is my typical girl?"

"Come on now. Vixens who like to be around money and well, I guess your muscular physique. She looks honest, sweet, and when she looks at you, her eyes sparkle as if she cares about you and not your money. What's the story?" He pours me a refill. I ran my finger around the rim of the glass, staring into the brown liquid.

"Where do I start?

"So, there is a story."

"She showed up at my apartment last year and I thought she was a guy wanting to rent my spare bedroom. Which was vacant due to the last renter leaving abruptly."

Max looked confused. "Oh, right. Cliff slept with Stacey. I'm glad she's gone, but clearly Jamie is not a guy."

"No, she's not. I received an email from what I thought was a guy named 'Jamie.' She thought she was responding to a girl named "Michaela". Max, I opened my door and saw her and something hit me in the middle of my chest. I didn't know her name but all I saw were two beautiful green eyes staring back at me and I knew I wanted to know everything about her. She is unlike any girl I have ever known. She is my future."

"Does she know how you feel?"

"We just recently became a couple."

Max rubs his chin, and then pours another drink for himself. "You're in love."

I nod in agreement. He comes from around the bar. "Look, I've known you a long time. I've seen girls, lots of girls, come and go with you. But this one has captivated you. Tell the woman how you feel. I bet she'll say the same thing to you."

I turn up my glass. "Thanks for the drink and the advice, but I'm going to find her."

"I'm sure Maci has told her plenty about you."

"I'm a little afraid of that."

*

Maci is talking and filling my glass with her specialty wine spritzer. I'm not sure how long it's been since the guys went to talk, but I've been told some really good stories about Michael that had me laughing, wanting more. She's now talking about shopping in town, restaurants, and a gathering they are going to tomorrow night that we should also attend when I feel an arm around my waist and a kiss on my cheek. Then Michael sits beside me, grabbing a chip.

"I've heard a lot of stories about you."

"Like what?"

Max goes around to Maci and gives her a squeeze. She smiles and bumps him with her hip.

"I told her about the time in the eleventh grade when you chose to bare all, running through the lunch room for $20. I also mentioned the time you shaved your body, put goats on the roof of the school, and the Victoria Smith incident in twelfth grade. Really juicy stuff and look sweetie, she's still here." She winks at Michael.

Max pipes in. "What about the bus we borrowed to free the dogs and cats from the shelter? Not sure why that one happened."

Maci puts her arms around Max and then looks at Michael.

"We miss those carefree days."

"I miss you guys, not the trouble we caused. Jamie, do you want to walk outside?"

"Yes. Maci, thank you for the spritzers."

"Sweetie, anytime, go, go enjoy your man. Michael, promise you won't take her away yet. I see that look in your eyes."

"Maci, what does that mean?"

"It means lust, but you both just got here! I want to talk more with Jamie."

Michael escorts me out onto an enormous deck facing the mountain with a fire pit and lights strung corner to corner.

I grab his hand. "She's a talker."

He leans on the rail. "Too much, I'm afraid."

"She gave me all the good stories and basically told me what I already know."

He leans into me. "Like?"

"She explained how you pushed your parents, tested the waters with girls, and basically played out your life dangerously through sports, friends, and pranks."

"How do you see me now?"

"A man who is strong, a good listener, and protects those he cares about. You are dedicated to your job and me. You make good choices and are supportive."

He kisses my shoulder. "It's because of you, my best choice ever."

*

The snow was beginning to fall on the drive back to the cabin and I wondered. *Could this place be any more magical?* We stand in front of the huge window, looking at the lights on the mountain. I'm wrapped in his arms leaning back against him.

"The party was fun."

"It was. Are you tired?"

I turn to face him. "No, not at all. In fact, turn around."

His left eyebrow goes up. "Why?"

"Just do it. It's all about trust."

He smiles, then turns, trying to peek over his shoulder.

"No peeking! I want you to count to ten."

He begins to count as I start taking off all my clothes, except for the polka dot lingerie. "Okay, you can turn around."

His eyes tell me so much and I feel my skin get warm just from a look. He lays his right hand on my hip, tracing the top of my underwear. His hand travels up my stomach to trace a few dots on the bra, then he hooks his finger in the strap, pulling me to him. He kisses my nose as his other hand comes up, supporting my neck.

"Do you remember what I said earlier?"

"That you picked this lingerie for you? But why?"

He scoops me up. "Let me show you."

*

I sit up in bed enjoying the smell of coffee and bacon. What is it with me and food? I crawl out of bed to freshen up in the bathroom. I pile my hair up on my head in a messy knot and grab a towel, wrapping it around me. I go looking for him and find the fireplace lit, music playing, and the most important person I know standing in the kitchen.

I stop suddenly. "What are you wearing?"

He spins to face me. "Good morning. It's an apron. I found it in the drawer."

"You're *only* wearing an apron." I walk over touching his back. He bends his head to give me a kiss.

"It's a small apron, but it shields my bare skin from the bacon popping."

"I like it. Maybe it should come home with us," I say playfully, before smacking him on his bare butt.

"Our math lesson went long into the night, so I figured we needed substantial food."

"You call what we did a math lesson?"

"Yes, my best lesson so far. Please go and have a seat. I set us up over by the fireplace."

I walk past him, pulling at his apron strings. He raises an eyebrow at me and I giggle and make my way over to the sofa. Shortly thereafter, he brings over a tray with food and sits next to me.

"Let's talk about our day. There's skiing, shopping, staying in…"

I wipe my mouth with a napkin. "Staying in is tempting, but I know you enjoy skiing, so I say let's do some more of that."

He tips up his coffee cup. "Are you sure?"

"Yes, oh naked one." I flip his apron.

"Be careful—I feel you have nothing on to protect you, except this towel."

I playfully smack at his hand. "Still frisky this morning, heh?"

"Always with you."

"Touché!"

"I'd like to ski with you today to see your form, your technique."

"There is no technique. Besides, your skills are on another level than mine. I'm good on the beginner's slope. We can meet up for lunch. Then maybe some sightseeing around town. You can show me some of your old haunts."

"Sounds like a good plan. But first I have to get you out of this towel; it's not appropriate for the slopes."

"And your apron?"

"I see your point." He stands up and strips it off walking down the hall to the bedroom.

He's not shy. "Wait for me."

*

We part ways after getting equipment, etc. He's on the more experienced slope and I head to the beginner/intermediate and meet up with one of my fellow skiers from yesterday who fell today and required the help of the rescue team. Luckily it was nothing serious and with a smile, she assured me she would be fine left in the care of "Hank" from the rescue team. I went up the mountain a few more times by myself. After an hour or so I head towards the lodge and run into Maci.

"Jamie, are you finished or going out to ski?"

"I've finished. Heading over to meet Michael for lunch."

"Well tonight we're all going to Joe's about 9:00. Talk to Michael and you guys come and meet us for booze, food, and dancing."

"I'll have him text Max if we are coming."

"Sounds good. I've got to run, I'll see you later."

I find Sondra's Café along with Michael sitting at a table drinking coffee. He stands to greet me. "How was your skiing?"

"It was good—I'm getting there." He pulls out my chair.

"Did you have fun?"

"No broken bones."

"I saw Maci before coming here. She invited us to Joe's tonight and mentioned dancing."

"We can go if you want. I hope you worked up an appetite."

Before I can answer him, our waitress comes over with my iced tea and two plates of sliders with fries.

"It's bison—very tender."

"They smell delicious. So, after this are we going exploring?"

"Yes. I will be your tour guide of my youth, the shops, and Ella's— they have the best ice cream."

"Count me in. It sounds wonderful."

After lunch, we enter a touristy shop and I purchase a postcard for Ruby. We keep walking down the street, going in and out of shops, until he ushers me into a little boutique. I stop.

"You want to come in here?"

"I want to buy you a dress."

I look around the store. "Michael, it looks expensive. Really, you don't have to."

"But I want to. You look and I'll look. Let's see what we find." I am reluctant at first, but he's so sweet to want to do it, so I accept his challenge. I catch glances of him over the racks looking serious, flipping through dresses. It was no time at all before he says my name. I turn to look for him. He's holding a navy blue skater dress.

"Well what do you think? It's okay if you don't like it."

"It's pretty."

"So, you like it?"

"Yes, I do." I reach out to feel the material.

191

"Will you let me buy this for you?"

I kiss him. "Yes of course. It's beautiful and I can wear it tonight."
He leaves to pay for the dress when a girl stops next to me.

"Does he have a brother? That dress cost $450. You are a lucky girl."

She's right. I'm lucky— not because of the dress, but because he
cares for me in the way he does. "Yes I am."

*

For Joe's tonight, I wear my new dress with nude strap heels.
Michael helps me off with my coat and takes my hand in his before entering
the bar. Back home, 42 is a bar for college students, with memorabilia on the
walls, video games, and one large bar. This place has two huge colorfully lit
bars, a dance floor, and lots of tables with linen tablecloths—very swanky.

"Do you like it?"

"I do."

"Let's get a drink."

We pass a group of ladies who are clearly waiting for him to walk
by. He's dressed in black slacks and a white button-down shirt, no tie, with a
jacket to match. He's all confidence without the arrogance, easy on the eyes,
and so sexy. I just tuck in close to him as he excuses our way to the bar. He
orders a beer and I get water.

"Are you sure you don't want something more? I can make it
happen."

"Maybe in a bit."

"Um, brace yourself—here she comes." He looks past me and I turn
around. Maci is heading in our direction holding a bottle in one hand and
glasses in the other, wearing a black skirt with a sheer purple blouse, and

once again heels that make her very tall. She leans in to plant a kiss on Michael's cheek a couple of times, then turns to hug me. She looks down at my glass and frowns.

"I see you're having a party of your own," Michael says.

"Michael, wherever I am, it's a party. But I knew your little hottie wouldn't order her own drink in here, so I brought her a little something." She turns to me. "Jamie, this dress is a beauty. It's a Lauren Oliver, isn't it? From her shop in town?"

"Yes, Michael picked it out. The material is unlike anything I've ever touched."

I look at him and wink.

"I love her stuff. Look, we know the guy who owns this bar. They stay open all night long and we are all going to have a good time, so take this glass." I go to say no, but she stops me.

"'No' is not a word we are using tonight. Turn it up." She tips the bottom of my glass with her hand.

"It's champagne."

"Good isn't it? Do you taste the strawberries?"

"I do."

She gives Michael the bottle and takes my hand, leading us to our table.

Max is there with a tray of four shots and two beers. He shakes Michael's hand and leans over to kiss my cheek.

"Jamie."

"Max."

"I hope you're ready to deal with Maci tonight; she's pumped up to get drunk and dance the night away." He hands me a shot, then gives one to everyone else. "Here's to a great evening with wonderful friends new and old." We tap our glasses together.

A song comes on and Maci pulls me to the dance floor. I knew I had to pace myself with the alcohol, but it looked like this train had pulled away from the station. Michael and I make a few trips around the bar and I meet a couple more of his friends. I'm approached by a girl in the bathroom who says she's into me and wanted to know if I would be interested in a threesome. After picking my chin up off the floor, I politely decline, heading out to find Michael.

"Excuse me sir, do you want to dance?" I ask, pulling him onto the dance floor. He pulls me into his arms, moving to the slow paced song.

"I was propositioned by a girl in the bathroom wanting to know if I was interested in a threesome."

"Interesting. What did you say?"

"I declined."

"Is that something you have thoughts about?"

"Not really, but she was cute. I'm not sure if she had the third person or she saw you with me. Either way it's a no."

"Good. I'm not interested in sharing my girl." On that note he dips me.

After a few more songs we both needed water so we went to the table. I sat down while he excused himself to the restroom.

While I wait for Michael to return, Max appears.

"May I sit down?"

"Sure." He's smiling with glassy eyes. "Are you alright?"

"I'm fine. A little drunk, but okay. Have you enjoyed your trip to Colorado?"

"Yes, it's an incredible place."

"I've been watching you with Michael. May I ask you a question?"

"Of course." I prop my elbows on the table and he moves a little closer to me.

"Do you have his back?"

"Yes, I would do anything for him."

"My old friend has fallen for you, real hard. I've known him a long time and he's never exhibited such behaviors with anyone else before."

"Behaviors? Like what?"

"He was reckless before. Always had a chip right here." He points to his shoulder. "But now, he's happy, speaking about the future, talking about you with stars in his eyes."

I smile, wondering where he's going with this.

"Do you love him?"

The words come very easily from my mouth.

"Yes, I love him."

Max stands up from his seat. "Good, 'cause he's standing right behind you. Tell him how you feel."

I turn on my stool to see Michael. He reaches up, grabbing the sides of my face and we take a moment, just looking at each other. Then I hear the words I've wanted to hear from him.

"I love you, I always have."

We kiss, a firm "don't-move-kiss," confirming our love for one another. His arms go around me, mine around him. He rests his forehead against mine.

"It feels good to say the words I have held for so long.

I needed you to be ready to hear them."

My whole body is tingling. "I've been ready but I wasn't sure it's what you wanted."

We kiss again before we're interrupted by Max, who pulls us apart.

"I hope you both remember who got all this love out in the open especially when you start naming babies."

We hug and thank him. Maci comes over with a server behind her carrying a tray of drinks.

"What's up guys?"

"I just opened the door for these two hot people to say, 'I love you.'"

Maci comes over to Michael. "You're finally ready to give that big heart away?"

"Yes. She's everything I want."

Maci hugs him and turns to me. "You're a lucky girl to have him love you, but I think he's equally lucky you love him. When she hugs me, all I can see are two dark brown eyes behind her that are my world.

After another hour or so we return to our cabin. We took another step tonight confirming our love for one another. Who knew three small words spoken to the right person could have such an impact? My heart has healed, his trust is renewed. In each other's arms we are a couple with many possibilities ahead of us.

Chapter 26

 ur flight was delayed, so we parked ourselves in chairs with hot coffee. Going through my phone, I look at the pictures I took in Colorado. "I think this one is my favorite."

He leans over to look. "When did that happen?"

"When we came back from dinner with Maci and Max our last night. Did you forget? You decided to take me to bed caveman style right out of the hot tub. I had just taken a pic of us in the hot tub and was able to snap one of your butt. It looks good."

He covers his face with his hand and laughs. "Really?"

"Yes, you have one of those bodies that screams touch me, kiss me, make love to me, and take my picture." He touches my cheek.

"Do you want to see the pics I took?"

My eyes dart in his direction, wondering what he took but our flight is called.

*

The plane lands on time and soon we're hailing a cab to Hopson College. After such a lavish vacation, it's easy to forget about our responsibilities at home, but I'm sure the drive back will refresh our memories. We crawl inside the car.

"Jamie, do you mind if we run by the 42 before going home?"

"No, is everything okay?"

He gives the cab driver the address and leans back in the seat, resting his hand on my leg.

"Pete texted earlier and I promised if it wasn't too late, that I would drop by."

I yawn. "Not a problem, you go, I go."

He rest his head on mine. "Best Christmas present my parents have ever given to me."

"It's one I'll never forget."

*

We pull up to the 42 about 10:30 pm, so people are just getting started. We stop first at the main bar. "Stuart, where's Pete?"

"He's in the kitchen. Glad to have you both back. How was Colorado?"

I peek around Michael. "Excellent."

"Well that smile explains it all."

Michael picks up our bags and we head to the kitchen to find Pete elbow deep in soapy water.

"Michael! Glad you're back. Now, can you unclog this old sink?" Pete reaches for a towel to dry his hands. Michael begins rolling up his sleeves after handing me his coat.

"Dude, really?"

"Yes, and now I can tell Jamie hi." He walks over and pulls me into a hug.

"How was the skiing?"

"A little difficult at first but the mountain views were spectacular."

"Good to hear and from the looks of those bags, you haven't been home yet?"

Michael dries his hands. "No, we're here for the papers and now the sink is unclogged."

Pete throws the towel in the bin. "Those are on your desk upstairs."

Michael reaches for Pete's hand. "Thanks for keeping an eye on things while I was gone."

"We're a team—besides you needed to get away. Maybe I'll take the next trip south."

"Sounds good. Just let me know." Michael looks at me. "Let's go up. Pete, will you have someone bring up coffee and donuts?"

"I can do that."

*

Upon entering the office, I sit down on the sofa, but not before looking at the changes made after the robbery. It stings my heart thinking back to that night. Broken items have been replaced, his computer system is updated, the safe is different, and the whole room has been painted. Michael sets the bags on the floor and goes over to his desk picking up the papers.

"Can I help?"

"Um, yes. Would you come over here please?"

"Sure. What are you reading?"

He takes my hand. "I don't want you to get mad, but do you remember the phone call I had a few days ago standing in the kitchen at the cabin?"

"Yes, why?"

"It was about this report." He hands it to me. I look down and see mine and Stacey's names on the paperwork.

"Jamie, it's about the altercation you had with her in the bar before we left on our trip."

I look over the report. It's from the Dean of Student Affairs about a hearing that's taking place tomorrow in their office at 4:00 in the afternoon.

"Are you serious?"

"Keep reading." I walk away from him while I read the paper.

"It states I was harassing her and being abusive while she was in the bar that night. She has witnesses to it all." I set the papers down. "None of what is stated is true. Why didn't you tell me when you found out?"

"I didn't want it to ruin your trip and there was nothing that was going to change before we came back. I did have Pete call the people who left statements on your behalf and he asked if they would attend the hearing. They all said yes. I'm sorry she went this far, but as the owner of the bar; I have to follow it through."

I put my hand on his chest. "You should have told me. But I understand why you didn't. I don't think I've ever had anyone dislike me this much."

"We'll put an end to this tomorrow."

"What should I expect at the hearing?"

"There will be a panel of students who will hear both sides and after reviewing the facts and hearing from the witnesses, they'll make their decision."

"Which could be?"

"Suspension being the worst, maybe probation."

"Ugh."

"It's protocol for me as a business owner with an incident involving students. Part of an agreement I signed a couple years ago. She went too far that night and the hearing is going to prove it."

*

We leave to go home nearly two hours after entering the bar. I walk in the apartment first wanting to be back in Colorado alone with just him.

"I need to check if I have any assignments for tomorrow. What about you?"

"I'm good. I checked on the plane."

"That was smart, what was I doing?"

"Sleeping."

He picks up the luggage. "Jamie, where do you want your bag?"

"My room please." He looks disappointed.

"I'll change in there, and then meet you back in your room."

"I was hoping you would say that."

"You have one dresser; I don't mind keeping my stuff in the other room."

"Well, I want to sleep wherever you are, so I'm open to either bedroom."

"Are you kidding me? Your bed is huge with layers of comfort not to mention the firm pillows." I glance over at him, smiling.

He laughs. "I sleep better with you as well."

He leaves my room for his and I pick up my phone, checking for assignments or notices. One class was canceled but the reading assignment was posted. That can wait until tomorrow. I look around my room knowing what I need to do. I find my toiletry bag, then head to his room. He's already in the bathroom brushing his teeth. I lay my bag down on his sink and find my toothbrush.

He spits in the sink. "Miss me?"

"You've ruined me; I can't even brush my teeth in my own bathroom."

"Suits me."

Chapter 27

*R*unning this morning is for the sole purpose of clearing my head for the hearing today. I want it all done and over, so my life can freely enjoy the happiness it now has. The past few days with Michael in Colorado lived up to every dream I ever had. I found someone to love and he loves me back, so enough of the outside bull bringing us down. I round the corner of the apartment complex wondering if he is still asleep. Entering the apartment, I grab a bottle of water, then walk to his bedroom. I remove my shoes and crawl up beside him. Suddenly he whips around, flipping me until I'm under him. "I was trying to…

"Surprise me?

"Yes."

"I would have gone running with you."

"I know, but I just needed to clear my head for today. You, Mr. Tucker, are the most distracting force in my life right now."

He buries his head in my neck. "You smell like the outdoors."

"Mix it with sweat— probably not sexy."

"You're wrong; you're very intoxicating to my senses. I wish I could change today for you."

"She's obsessed with you. How do I deal with an obsessed woman when it comes to my boyfriend? She wants you and will stop at nothing to get you."

His finger outlines my jaw. "You're clenching your teeth."

"Because she makes me mad."

"She was never this obsessed with me, unless my wallet was out. Stay in bed with me, let me try my hand at relaxing you." He snuggles in close to me, showering me with soft kisses.

"As much as I would love to stay in bed with you while you work magic on me, I have to get to class." He lets out a sigh and rolls off me.

I crawl out of bed. "You could join me in the shower."

He jumps out of bed. "Right behind you."

*

My classes go smoothly after being out for break. I stop to grab a quick coffee and then I'm off to my professor's office before heading to my hearing later. Professor Stower left me an email message to stop by today, because he had good news for me. I'm curious as to what it could be, so I enter the Wick Building and head for his office. His assistant asks me to wait till he's off the phone, which only takes only a few minutes.

"Jamie, come in, please have a seat." His office is filled top to bottom with books, a couple computer screens, and a big oak desk that's filled with many papers and more books. I take off my backpack and sit.

"Jamie, have you considered what you want to do when you graduate?"

"A little, but nothing definite."

He leans back in his chair with his hands behind his head. "I noticed last semester that you were more involved in the class discussions with good ideas. Your presentations were well thought out, your organizational skills, along with your ability to communicate with the other students was outstanding. I have a friend who owns a business here in town and he comes to me every year for intern applicants. He wants a business major; I want you to think it over, take this folder, and read over the company bullet points, then let me know if you have any questions. It might be a good start for your career after college."

"I will. Thank you, Professor Stower. Thanks for putting my name in for the position." I pick up my backpack and the folder, leaning over his desk to shake his hand. "Thank you again."

"You are welcome."

I leave his office a little surprised but elated that I was chosen. This is quite an opportunity, but it would keep me really busy along with the extra classes I'll take over the summer. I will have to speak with Michael about my hours at 42, but right now I have just enough time to go home and change for the hearing.

*

Riding up to the second floor in the Parks Building, my nerves are little edgy, but I know I'm right on how the altercation went down that night. The elevator door opens, and I immediately see Michael.

"You look great."

"Tell me she isn't coming, that she dropped all this, and we're done and can go home."

Then the elevator doors open, too late. She comes out but not alone. Michael takes my hand and we proceed inside the room and take a seat. I'm in pants with a white blouse and Stacey is wearing a white dress with a plunging neckline, along with brown spiked heeled booties. She knew what she needed to do—exploit her assets, so they won't listen to her ridiculous account of events. She also arrived with two friends who were there that night as well. Administrative assistant versus sorority sex kitten— let the fight begin. Caleb walks in and sits on my side. Stacey shoots him a look that I guess was supposed to drive him to her side, though he doesn't budge. My own witnesses show up and I thank them for taking time to come out for me. The gavel hits the table as the complaint is read. She's called forward first.

Stacey starts by saying I'm jealous of her and Michael's past relationship and that we had a confrontation early that day at our sorority house that left her concerned that I might try and get even with her. She said that night at the bar I was lazy, rude, and abrupt with her. All I had to do was clean off the table, but I was belligerent.

If I didn't know how awful she could be I might feel sorry for her. She takes out a tissue to wipe her eyes. *What the heck is going on? She clearly has a personality disorder.*

I look at Michael, who shakes his head. They call up her witnesses to get their account of the incident. They're also dressed to catch the eye of the panel sitting before us. They each tell a story that's fabricated, just like hers.

Finally it's my turn. I stand and recount my version of the events that evening. I do not bring up situations that didn't happen inside the bar. I go over each encounter with her that night and describe the fight. I even show them a picture of my bruised, swollen face. They call up my witnesses and then call Michael to their table. When they're done, Michael turns and finds his seat next to me. They talk amongst themselves for about five minutes, then called us both up.

"Ladies, you are here today, due to a filed complaint about an altercation at the 42 bar near campus. We have come to the conclusion that this was a misunderstanding. We have determined there is no cause for anyone to be suspended or reprimanded for the incident." They look at her. "Mr. Tucker is an outstanding college senior and reputable bar owner who clearly is not charging you for the altercation in his bar. Ms. Morgan, the same goes for you and nothing will appear in your permanent files."

I nod and say thank you. They slam down the gavel.

Stacey stands there with her hands on her hips. "Are you serious? This isn't right. She attacked me, and you do nothing?"

They walk away without acknowledging her statement.

"So that is it?" Clearly annoyed, she looks over at us, addressing her statement to Michael. "This is all wrong. I'm not done with this." She gathers her stuff off the table and then tells her friends it's time to leave. Before departing, she comes back to us, running her well-manicured finger down the front of Michael's shirt, which makes my blood boil.

"You know we are good together. The day is coming where all you will want is me. Just wait. You'll see."

He steps close to her. "Stay away from me, from Jamie and the 42. Whatever you have brewing in your head stops today. Do you understand?"

She finally walks away, but not before looking over at Caleb. She smiles, blowing him a kiss. "You have my number."

He holds up his hand shaking his head no then looks over at me. I shake my head in disbelief walking over to my witnesses to thank them for coming today. They all tell me it was all her fault, and they were glad it got dismissed. Caleb walks up as they're leaving.

"She put on quite the show, huh? Look thank you for coming and doing this today."

"Jamie she is nuts plain and simple and I don't think she's done. It's like she's snapped. On a higher note, how was Colorado?"

"Amazing! A place I would like to travel to again."

Michael steps up to address Caleb. "Do you want to grab some food?"

"I can't. I'm in a study group that's meeting in ten minutes. But thanks for the offer."

Michael and I walk outside, but I have one last question.

"What did you say to those guys?"

He smiles. "Do you really want to know?"

"Yes, I do."

He slides his hands in his front pockets. "They asked if I kicked you both out that night. I said I kicked Stacey out of the bar for good, and I went home with you. They said that was a good choice and that everything was being dismissed. They knew she was crazy from her outfit and performance."

I put my arms around his waist. "I'm so done with her. Are there anymore ex's that might come out to attack me?"

"No, you're safe. How about some dinner?"

"As long as we can take dessert home."

He squeezes me closer to his side. "Dessert in bed?"

"Yes."

"Take out it is."

Chapter 28

I'm getting ready for my interview with ECON, the company Professor Stower recommended to me by researching them online and going over the notes he gave me. It's a nonprofit helping in the community, throughout the state, and with a couple of international projects getting attention in the news. The front door opens and Michael's soaked from the rain and still in workout clothes, holding a bag of Chinese food and a rose. I rush over to grab the wet bag before it lands on the floor.

"Let me help you." I took the bag as his free hand cups my neck to steady me for a long hello kiss.

"It's like the sky opened up. I'll hop in the shower and be back in ten minutes. This is for you." He hands me the rose.

"Thank you. It smells sweet."

He goes around the corner, down the hall, peeling off his shirt, as he calls back, "Just like my girl."

I busy myself setting up date night, putting out food, and placing my rose in a small glass when Michael returns from his shower.

"Today was very busy—it's good to be home. How was your day?"

"I spent time getting ready for my interview, finished a drawing for class, and thought of you."

"Good thoughts, I hope."

I raises an eyebrow, popping a dumpling in his mouth. "Always."

We talk about my work shifts changing to be able to take the internship if offered and me maybe even stepping back from classes or only taking one or two over the summer. We both agree as neither want a repeat from last summer. He talks about the upcoming meeting with his dad that will decide what happens after he graduates—and what it might mean for us as a couple. Big decisions, but I know we will make it work. After dinner, there's chocolate silk pie, a movie, and us. No drama, no phones, just a normal evening enjoying each other.

*

Michael

The next day my parents were coming to town about a new jobsite. Mom decided to visit me while Jamie was in class. I was looking forward to seeing her, but not the meeting later with Dad going over financial reports for the bar or plans for my future.

Mom is in the apartment for five minutes and sees me pacing the floor in front of her. She raises her hands. "Please sit down and talk to me. Why are you anxious?"

"I have lots to tell Dad at our meeting tonight but mostly about my future with Jamie." I sit down beside her. "Mom, I love her."

My mother says nothing right away. "How does she feel about you?"

"She loves me. I can see marriage, kids, maybe a house in the 'burbs." She looks down at her hands then back at me.

"Mothers dream of the day their children find someone special. I'm just happy for you and for Jamie. She's a lovely girl who would do anything for you. I like seeing you looking towards your future, wanting more for yourself."

"I never thought caring for someone would mean so much to me."

"Well I can see she does. No one gets to say what your future will be except you, including your father. He will understand, given some time."

My phone vibrates on the table. "Excuse me, it's him."

After a brief conversation, I hang up the phone, tossing it on the table. She knows the call is not good but they never are. Our relationship may be past the point of repair.

"Do you think it ever mattered to him what I wanted?"

She comes over and lays her hand on my arm. "You want acceptance from your father, you always have but you need to stand up, state what you want, and then go after it. Let him know what's important to you. Your dad and I weren't high school or college sweethearts. He was at the firm I worked at on a temporary contract. I was called in to take minutes at the meeting he was attending. When I looked up waiting to start, he was staring at me. His eyes were dark, looking right at me, and I began to blush. He had such an intense look: handsome, determined. When the meeting was over, he asked me out."

"You said yes?"

"I did. On our first date I expressed my desire of wanting a business of my own."

"You?"

"Yes, I was disciplined, determined, and loved working just like him. We had only dated eighteen months when he asked me to marry him, right after signing a lease on his first building. We married six months later, and I was pregnant one year to the date. In fact, I told him I was pregnant on our first anniversary."

"Not in his career plan I'm sure."

"No. I worked until it was time to take maternity leave. But having you changed my heart and going back was no longer my priority. Your dad approached parenthood like a company, which caused a strain between us. I settled into my role as a mother, and he managed our growing business. Believe me, sweetheart. I see the toll it has taken on the two of you, but I know he loves you and one day he will see you and who you are." She reaches up and places a hand on my cheek, then pulls me in a hug. "I have to go. I hope Jamie can meet us for dinner tonight."

"I hope so too."

Jamie

Walking into the living room, I fix the strap to my shoe, then look at him holding a tie in his hand.

"Sorry. I hope we won't be late. Are you wearing that?" I point at the tie.

"You're looking lovely tonight."

"Thank you." I reach for the tie. "I vote no."

I toss it on the sofa.

"I'm glad you made it back for dinner tonight with my mother. As far as I know my father won't be there because of his meeting."

"What if he surprises you?"

"What and show up unexpectedly, asking questions and talking on his phone? Maybe."

"Well, let me know when you want to leave because you and I, along with my black lace underwear, will come home."

I grab his hand, leading him to the door.

"Seriously? You tell me this right before dinner with my mother."

"Are you thinking about your meeting with your dad?"

"No."

"Good. Mission accomplished."

The walk over to the restaurant is a good one with us stopping a couple of times to steal kisses. As we approach the end of the sidewalk, we glance both ways, then step off. Out of nowhere, a black SUV appears, almost hitting us. I would have taken the impact directly, but Michael pulled me away and is now cursing at the driver. Two other people were behind us but also stepped out of the way just in time.

"Jamie, are you okay?"

"Yes, I never saw them coming. Are you okay?"

"Yes, I'm fine. What is wrong with people not paying attention?" He puts his arms around my shoulders. It shakes us both, but we turn to the other couple, asking if they're okay and if they saw the license plate. They didn't, so we head to the restaurant.

We enter seeing his mom, but she's not alone. Mr. Tucker has joined her and is on the phone. I squeeze Michael's hand. "Just give the word."

His mom speaks first. "Jamie, it's so good you could join us. Your dress is so cute." She gives me a hug.

"Thank you." She goes to greet Michael as Mr. Tucker sticks out his hand to me.

"Jamie, nice to see you again."

"Thank you, sir, I'm glad you could make it."

"Yes, last minute change of plans." He holds out his hand to Michael.

"Son."

"Dad."

After we're all seated, the waitress comes over to take our drink orders. Almost immediately his dad starts throwing questions Michael's way about the profits report on the 42. He squeezes my leg under the table and I place my hand over his, wrapping it around his arm as he relaxes his grip.

"Michael your last semester will be done before you know it. How are the applications coming? Any responses back yet? I feel you should've had some news already. I hope it's not your first year here that's delaying those responses. It wasn't your best." He clears his throat. "I hope you thought about what I said earlier today, that law would be a smart career decision for you. I could make a few calls."

"Not necessary."

Tension is thick and both men pick up their beer glasses.

Mr. Tucker takes a sip, then turns to me. "Jamie, what is your major?"

"Business maybe, I'm not real sure yet."

"What do you want to do with that?"

"I'm still mulling it over."

"What does your family think? Do you have people to guide you? Your dad must have suggestions for you."

Mrs. Tucker laid her hand on his arm. "Harrison."

Michael stiffens in his chair as I answer his question. "I'm the only one in my family. My mom passed away when I was five, my dad less than two years ago. I have no siblings, no aunts or uncles. As for planning my future, I don't have the answers and right now I am focused on my academics, my job and building relationships." I lean into Michael's arm.

Mr. Tucker sees the gesture and says nothing for a moment. Then he looks at his son, like he just figured out something was different between us. "I'm sorry Jamie, Laura did tell me."

His phone vibrates, and he glances at it. "Jamie you may want to talk with someone who has knowledge in real life experiences. Young people struggle with money when they first start out after college with loans, living expenses, and poor decision making. Sometimes what's right now can be detrimental later. Please, excuse me." He leaves the table. Michael stands up, then pulls out my chair.

He looks at his mom, apologizing. "I'm sorry we won't be staying. Will I see you before you leave town?" His mother nods. He takes out money, leaving it on the table to pay for our meal that never arrived. I turn my attention to the woman who's being left at the table to deal with what just happened.

"It was nice to see you again, Mrs. Tucker."

She just smiles. She's probably felt this way many times when being with both her husband and son. Mr. Tucker comes back to the table. "Did something come up?"

Michael pauses for a moment. "Yes. Will I see you at 42 later or did that call change our meeting?"

His dad sits down, turning up his glass. "No change and I hope all the reports are in order."

"Of course."

Michael stands holding my coat. I glance at his mother who is watching her husband, he is looking at his son. *What big event will it take to get them back to being a father and a son?* We leave the restaurant taking only a few steps when he stops.

"I apologize for my father. He's all business, no heart."

"It's fine."

He starts walking again taking my hand. "I know he's smart when it comes to business, clearly his wealth proves that. But when it comes to feelings, he has none. From what you've told me, your dad put you first and still worked hard to make a life for his family. I'm done trying to live like he wants."

"Show him the passion you have behind your decision and then maybe he'll understand."

"We shall see."

*

I spend the next three and a half hours writing my paper while Michael has his meeting at the 42 with his dad. I must have fallen asleep because I awake to a noise outside my room. I look up to see him pulling his sports bag out of the way picking up the lamp. I turn on my light.

"Are you okay?"

"Sorry, I tripped over my gym bag and fell into the table." He takes off his shoes awkwardly which tells me he is tipsy.

"How was the meeting?"

217

He enters my room.

Undoing his belt then pulls down his pants, leaving them on the floor. He heads to the bathroom. "I'll be right back."

When he reappears, I pull back the sheet. "Join me."

He crawls in, kissing my cheek, smelling of toothpaste.

"Did you finish your paper?"

"Yes."

He lies back. "Good." He's still smiling with his eyes shut.

"Do you want to talk?"

"Not right now." Propping his head up on one of his folded arms, he begins to talk. "Where do I start? He comes in bringing a bottle of scotch, complimenting me on hiring Pete years ago, making the changes inside the bar that were needed, profits and the employee turnover. He sets down a glass for me and one for himself. Then it went downhill."

"What do you mean?"

"He began to break down my four years at Hopson—how he thinks I'm too young to be in a serious relationship, that I should get my career up and going first. I presented my proposal and he took it but said he would have his lawyers look over it. He then left, and I stayed for a few more rounds of the expensive scotch."

"How did you get home?"

"Campus bus, which I've not taken since my freshman year."

"I'm sorry it didn't go well."

"It's pretty normal but after tonight and what he said, I'm done. He can do what he feels is the right thing and from this point until the day I graduate, I'll do the same." He leans over, placing his hand on my cheek. "We'll be just fine." He lays back and closes his eyes.

I shut off the light, sliding down beside him as he puts an arm around me, kissing my head. He whispers, "I won't stop trying."

"I know you won't."

Chapter 29

I walk into a tall building made of grey stone with lots of windows facing towards a large, well landscaped pond with a fountain. I see a gentleman sitting at the front desk, who is reading something on a clipboard.

"Excuse me."

"Yes, may I help you?"

"I have a 2 pm interview with Steven Palmer with ECON."

He looks at his clipboard. "Your name?"

"Jamie Morgan."

"Yes, I have you down. Sign here and put this on." He hands me a badge.

"You will go down this hall to the elevator. ECON's offices are on the third floor."

"Thank you."

"Good luck."

The elevator doors open, and I step out. There's another desk, this time with an older lady with white hair and black rimmed glasses.

"May I help you?"

"I'm Jamie Morgan."

"Yes, please take a seat. May I get you a water?"

"No, thank you." I sit in a white leather chair surrounded by more white furniture and a large coffee table. I realize my hands are nervously rubbing my binder, which holds my resume of sorts.

"Ms. Morgan, Mr. Palmer will see you now. Please follow me." She opens a door leading to a conference room. Seated inside are three men, one of whom walks over to me.

"Ms. Morgan, nice to finally meet you in person. I'm Mr. Palmer. Your professor has all good things to say about you. Please have a seat and I can introduce you to everyone you might work with while here."

I take my seat next to Mr. Palmer. They start asking questions about me, my thoughts on the future, and we go over information about the company and the internship. About 45 minutes later, I'm done with the interview and a quick tour of the company. With a bottle of water in hand, I leave feeling good. I pass the ECON sign downstairs and touch it for good luck.

*

I enter the apartment, setting down my purse along with the new dress I bought on the way home. I fill a glass with water, then head out onto the balcony, taking a long sip. I lean my head back, taking in the smell of the outdoors and relishing the warm breeze. A "hi" breaks me out of my trance. I look to the right and a guy I've never seen before is standing on the next balcony, holding a beer.

"Hi."

"I didn't mean to startle you. I'm Josh—I just moved into this apartment."

"Oh, my name is Jamie. I live here with my boyfriend Michael. Are you a student?"

"No, I graduated a few years ago. I work as an Auditor at Simmons Bank. You attend Hopson?

"Yes, and so does Michael." I hear the sliding door open behind me.

"Hey you," says Michael, grabbing me tight around my waist. He nuzzles my neck tickling my skin. "Are you hungry?"

I giggle. "Yes, starving."

"Well let's fix that."

"Wait, I want you to meet our new neighbor. Michael, this is Josh."

Josh reaches out his hand. Michael does the same, but doesn't remove the other hand from my waist. "Do you attend Hopson?"

"I graduated a few years ago."

"There have been some changes."

"Yes. Windsor Hall is different and the soccer field has moved. Well, don't let me keep you guys from dinner."

Michael takes my hand, ushering me inside with his other hand. "You should come by the 42 Bar at the circle; we work there most days."

"Thanks, I might stop by."

I glance back at Josh still on the balcony. "He seems nice."

Backing me over to the sofa, Michael kisses me down the front of my blouse. I giggle saying his name as he pushes me and I fall onto the sofa.

"He's okay. I'm going to shower and then you can fill me in on your interview." With a quick kiss, he leaves only to come back. "Or we can delay dinner."

I throw a pillow at him. "Go shower!" He smiles then leaves. I love his playfulness and he's so charming. I get off the sofa following him down the hall unbuttoning my blouse. Who am I kidding he is my weakness.

We decide on burgers and go to our favorite little hole in the wall. I fill him in on my interview at ECON while we devour our dinner. He orders a slice of chocolate cake in celebration of my possible new internship while I excuse myself to the bathroom. When I return, Stan is talking to Michael.

"Stan! Where have you been? We've missed you!"

He picks me up in a bear hug. "You know, it could have been me you fell in love with, not this gorilla. You're looking sweet, so I guess he is doing something for you. I was just telling Michael that my dad got hurt, so I went home.

"Is he okay?"

"He's doing well now. We're having a keg party at the boat house Saturday, and you both need to come. You know, just be college students. Please come or I will hunt you down and drag you there." He kisses my cheek then slaps Michael on the shoulder. "I got to go, see you Saturday."

Michael puts payment on the table. "Stan really wanted to date you when you first came to Hopson. He crushed hard on you."

"He never asked me out. Was that because of you?"

"Yes, actually. I felt you needed friends because you were going through a hard time."

I wrap my arms around him. "You've always looked after me."

He tightens his arms around me. "I always will."

*

The next couple of days have flown by, but now Friday is upon us. I'm getting dressed for work at the 42, checking my phone for a message from ECON, but nothing. I grab my backpack and pull the door shut behind me. When I turn, I bump into Josh and drop my phone on the concrete.

"Josh, I'm so sorry—my mind is somewhere else."

"It's fine." He picks it up. "Protective covers do come in handy. What had your attention?"

"An internship."

"Waiting to see if you got it?"

"Yes. But right now my other job is waiting. You should come by later."

"I might just do that. I have some time before my meeting. May I walk with you?"

"Um, sure."

He walks me to the front door of the 42, where I am left wondering about him. He asked questions about me and Michael the whole walk over. I tried to change the conversation, but it always came back to us. He seems nice, but I am not ready to give that kind of information to anyone. Still, why is he that interested?

Chapter 30

$\mathcal{I}$ t's Saturday morning and we decide to run together and then get breakfast at Dot's. The rest of the morning will be taken up with laundry and cleaning which is not glamorous but needed. About 12:30, we sit down to eat lunch.

"What's your take on the new neighbor?"

I hand him the mustard. "Josh, what do you mean?"

"He seems to never have friends over and he's overly interested in you."

"Really?"

"When you were on the balcony reading the other night—before I came out to join you—he was leaning on the balcony rail staring over at you. Then he left as soon as I came out."

"He was probably looking at the girl down from us because she usually wears next to nothing. Besides he's asking me about you; maybe he's interested in strong and sexy instead."

"So, you think I'm sexy after cleaning the toilet?"

"Very much so."

"You must love me."

"I do."

"Well I'm going to keep my eye on him."

I finish chewing my bite of sandwich. "We could introduce him around the 42, put his mind on someone else other than you." He tosses a chip at me.

"How about a movie and a nap after lunch?"

"Sounds wonderful."

*

The party at the boat house is going strong. We're late due to a problem at work, but we're here now. Michael touches my elbow, stopping me. He has that look on his face.

"I know what you're going to say."

"You do, huh?"

"I promise to forget about ECON and be a carefree college student. But you have to promise to do the same."

He kisses me. "So, I get to cop a feel, steal kisses, and encourage drinking so I can get you back to my place. Is that right?"

"Yes. My part tonight is to tease you, show you but not show you my boobs and drink beer hoping you will take me to your place."

"Exactly." We shake on our plans for the night when my phone vibrates.

I read it. "Um, Caleb says he has information for me and wants to meet."

Michael gives me the raised eyebrow. "Right. No drama tonight." I text back that I'll call him tomorrow. Putting my phone away, we walk in search of the keg.

This party has pool, beer and poker games in full force. We mingle together then split off—he goes with the boys and I go with the girls. After a while there is a loud game of poker going on, with the boys smoking cigars as they wear their caps backwards and laugh at each other's jokes. I watch my boyfriend be free of future decisions, his dad, work responsibilities, and enjoy the party being a student. He needs this and I am buzzing, in need of water to drink or to splash on my face. In the bathroom I find Bethany throwing up.

"You okay? What do you need?" I move over, holding back her hair.

"Just promise me not to tell Derek because he will want me to go home and I'm having fun."

"Okay, but only water for you." She picks up her fingers in an okay sign. I go out to let her freshen up and to get us water from the cooler. Michael is standing at the keg refilling his cup, so I slide in front of him. He stops pouring.

I take the nozzle. "May I pour for you?"

"That works for me. Now my hands are free to touch you."

I turn to face the keg and his hands are now on the top of my jeans, where he hooks his thumbs. I can feel his warm fingers on my skin under my shirt.

"Is Bethany okay?"

"Yes, too much beer not enough water. Did Derek see her?"

"No." He points towards the sofa. "A little out himself. How are you?"

"A good buzz. I heard the girls were joining for strip poker—are we playing?" I turn to face him.

His lips come down on mine, barely touching them as he smiles. He tilts my chin up, putting his other hand in my hair tilting my head back so he can pursue his mission of my mouth. When he's done, I can't move, I don't move. I open my eyes and look into his.

"Okay, no strip poker for me."

"We can play at home."

I raise up on my toes to kiss his neck, then tug on his ear with my teeth. He lets out a purring noise, deep in his throat. Then we hear Stan.

"STOP, enough! Some of us are single and going home alone. This display of affection is not helping us. That kiss was a little R rated."

"You told us to be college students and I found the girl I'm taking home."

I look over at Stan. "Are you hungry?"

"Yes, I want what you both are having." He grabs my hand. "Taco Hut, here we come!" He pulls me away from Michael towards the door, yelling behind him.

"Anyone else hungry?"

*

Most of us are strolling down the sidewalk heading to Taco Hut in search of food to put in our stomachs along with the beer. The girls are walking behind the guys who are making us laugh at their antics. One falls into a bush, two roll into the street from playing leap frog. We start cheering when we hear the music at Taco Hut and they're already busy with other food deprived students.

228

"Jamie, do you want the usual?"

"Yes, thank you."

*

We find tables, sit, and gorge ourselves with tacos. About 4:15 in the morning, we decide to part ways and head home. Stan has met a girl from Mathews College here visiting her friend, so with him busy, leaving is easy. We're talking about how much fun we had when my phone vibrates, with an unknown number. I put it away.

"Is it another one?"

"Yes, unknown."

"Just like before? Are you getting more?" Right then, it vibrates again: unknown. Michael takes the phone to answer it.

"Hello, who is this? Stop calling this number. We are monitoring this phone and we will know who you are. They hung up." He hands me my phone back. "Let me know if you keep getting calls. We might need to change your number."

"Agreed."

We finally arrive at the apartment and he stops holding up his arm in front of me. He puts his finger to his lips. My eyes go to what he's looking at: the slightly open door to the apartment.

"Jamie, call the police and stay here."

I grab for his arm. "Michael, don't. Let's call them together."

He touches my face. "Please stay here." He walks in the apartment unarmed.

I call 911, telling them what is happening and give the address. They make me stay on the line, but I want to go inside. I move closer to the door when they finally arrive. I wave to them then turn back to the apartment, when I see Michael coming out. He tells them the apartment was empty, but wants to follow them inside to show them what he found. He looks at me.

"I'll be right back."

I wait for him to return, with all kinds of thoughts running through my head. He comes to the door.

"Jamie, come inside."

I'm sure my face tells him I'm in a panic and he takes my hand telling me what's happened.

"The apartment has been broken into so we can't touch anything yet." We approach an officer holding a pen and pad while another officer comes out of the back of the apartment to stand with us.

"Miss Morgan, we want you to go into your bedroom and let us know if anything is missing but don't touch your things yet. Officer Pittman will go with you."

I walk into my room and see my bed has been torn apart. The drawers are open and there are clothes thrown all over. The nightstand is empty and all the items are on the floor. The medicine cabinet in the bathroom has also been trashed. I can't tell if anything is missing because of the mess. I turn to go back into the living room.

"Jamie, they want to ask you some questions like they asked me."

"Sure."

"I'm Sergeant Rose. Could you state your full name please?"

"Jamie Carson Morgan."

"Miss Morgan, you are a renter here at this address. Is this correct?"

"Yes, sir."

"Ma'am, have you had any problems with anyone lately? An ex-boyfriend, coworker, or neighbor. Mr. Tucker told me about his ex-girlfriend who lives here on campus that she has been giving you some grief, not letting go easily."

I look at Michael. "She is a little over the top in her actions but to break in and do all this, I just don't know. I've received a few calls on my phone lately that are coming up as unknown. In fact I received some tonight."

"We can try and trace the location of the calls, but you'll have to come down to the station tomorrow. But for tonight we have a few more things to do here then we can be out of your way."

Michael shakes his hand.

The officers go about doing their job and my stomach feels uneasy. Is it from the booze or the fact our home has been invaded?

"Michael, we don't bother anyone. Why do these things happen to us?" Do you think it could be Stacey?"

"I'm not sure but the police will let us know what they find. Let's go to a hotel tonight. Maybe we can get some sleep, have breakfast, and then go to the station with your phone later. They'll put a temporary lock on the door. What do you think?"

Looking around I agree with him to leave the apartment.

We enter the hotel about 5:30 in the morning and I go about pulling the curtains shut. We stopped at the gift shop to pick up toothbrushes, since we couldn't take anything with us. I walk into the bathroom and watch him take them out of the wrappers. My eyes fill with tears.

"Jamie what can I do?"

I shake my head not able to say anything.

"Let's brush, then go to bed. Whether we sleep or not."

I go about washing my face and brushing my teeth, then join him in the bed.

His steady breathing and his arms around me lulls me asleep, only I wake me up some time later from a dream where a stranger is holding me by my waist as I kick and scream for him to let go. I see Michael slumped on the floor, but I can't get away and then a door shuts and I lose sight of him. I sit up in bed, breathing heavily and look to my left, where I find him sleeping. I crawl out of bed, then head to the bathroom. Looking in the mirror, I see that my eyes are puffy from crying, so I turn on the water and splash cold water on my face.

I'm handed a towel. "You tossed and turned the whole time."

I scrunch up my face. "I'm sorry."

"Don't be. Our apartment was broken into. It's disturbing."

"I woke up from a dream where I was being held by a man and you were lying on the floor. I couldn't get to you."

He pulls me to him. "I'm right here with you and we are going to be fine. Let's shower then grab breakfast. Sergeant Rose left me a message so we can go to the station after we eat."

"Do you think they know more?"

"He didn't say but at least maybe we can find out more about the calls you've been getting."

"I hope so."

Chapter 31

eturning home after more questions at the police station, the task ahead of us is daunting, but I won't feel better until it is all cleaned up. We decide to work individually to get it done faster but turning on the light brings reality to life. I pull the sheets and comforter off the bed and lay them next to the door. I look under the mattress and under the bed and find nothing but broken glass from frames. Next, I start putting items back into the nightstand but notice nothing missing. Next is the top drawer of the dresser—some clothes are in, some out but nothing strange. The second drawer is the same, but the third drawer proves to be different. My journals were in this drawer and they're missing. A stack of three tied with ribbon. Gone. Who would want something so private? I call out to Michael.

He comes down to my room. "What's wrong?"

"My journals aren't here."

"Maybe you took them out and put them somewhere else?"

"No, they were here. I've checked all the drawers. Why would someone take them? One of them my mom started for me when she got sick that last time. I remember one day I was cleaning out my room and I think I was about 12 years old when I found the journal with written entries from her to me in the closet." I throw back my head. "This is insane." I look at him concerned. "Phone numbers and addresses were in one of them for Ruby,

Susan and even the lawyer." I go to the closet looking for my dad's briefcase but it's also gone. "The letter from the lawyer and the contents from the box he gave me are inside the case." I sit down on the bed.

He sits beside me. "I don't have answers for you, other than maybe they thought more was in the case."

"So you feel all this is weird too."

"I do. Let me help you in here and then we can go finish mine."

We do just that, putting my room back together and even start a load of laundry. His room is next, where he had also piled sheets by the door.

"So far the picture of us in Colorado is gone. I looked under everything, thinking it flew out of the broken frame but nothing. Oh, and my college ring, my watch that was given to me by my grandfather, and some team metals. Also an odd assortment." His phone vibrates. "It's my insurance company."

"Go, take it. I'll be right here."

I walk into his bathroom and see he's cleaned up everything. Looking up, I see the fear, the realness of what a person feels when an intruder enters your safe place. *Enough of the pity party, Jamie. Get mad, fight back because fear is weakness and I won't let this wreck me.*

I go to find Michael. "Is everything okay?"

"Yes, they needed some information. Let's finish and then I will call Sergeant Rose. After that, I'll make my spaghetti for dinner. Sound good?"

"Okay. Only if I can assist."

"I would love that."

After about 30 minutes or so, we left his room to prepare our dinner. One tomato sauce splattered t-shirt later, we were done and enjoying our labor of love. I also received a phone call from Lidia in HR at ECON offering me a position to start Monday and apologizing for the delay in getting back with me. I accepted the position gladly.

Going to bed that night took longer for us to fall asleep. I heard every little sound and he felt every flip that I made.

Chapter 32

*W*e implement safety procedures suggested by Sergeant Rose and monitor our credit cards, bank accounts, and I notified Ruby and Susan. Insurance is filed for Michael's missing items but my personal items have not shown up anywhere. A few weeks have passed since starting my new job at ECON and I'm loving the work and grateful for the opportunity.

Sipping green tea with honey reading over an assignment for class, I notice Josh on his balcony talking on the phone. He's clearly agitated with the person on the other end. He tosses the phone in a chair, then disappears only to come out with a beer, downing it in seconds. I head out to check on him and I guess the sound of the sliding door startles him because he shoots a wild eyed look at me.

"I saw you from inside and you look upset. Everything alright?"

He hesitates, forcing a smile. "Work."

"Can't leave it behind, huh?"

He looks down at his bottle. "Well, not this part. Do you want a beer?"

"No thanks. Do you want to talk about it?"

He sets the bottle on the table walking to the balcony railing between us. "Your eyes are a beautiful green color. A man could get lost in them. Can I take your picture?" He turns to find his phone.

"I need to get back inside. I hope whatever is going on works out."

"It will. Goodnight, Jamie."

I close the sliding door, looking over at him. He smiles, then walks inside. Over the next couple of weeks, he's distant and I surely didn't approach him on the balcony alone as the last situation was awkward enough. One night, Michael notices him hit the door outside his apartment with his fist, so he asks if he can help. Josh says nothing other than, "I got to go." He goes inside his apartment, slamming the door behind him. He didn't show up this week for the game either. He is different now, but why? Michael called him wanting to meet but he said he had no time.

*

Tonight is Open Mic night at 42 and a big crowd has formed inside. I make my way straight to the clock in station and see Pete.

"How's it going tonight? Nice crowd out there." He gives me a look.

"What's wrong? Staff call out?"

"You and Michael are friends with that guy Josh, right?"

"Yes, but he has been distracted lately and we don't know why."

"Well he's been here for a while drinking, talking loud, and is about to get cut off or thrown out."

"That's weird."

"Do you want to talk to him? I'm sure you know Michael got delayed with a flat tire on the team bus."

"Yeah, he texted me. I'll try."

"Look, if he gives you any trouble, tell Stuart, and he'll be removed."

"I will." I approach Josh cautiously, remembering our last encounter. "Hey Josh."

He spins around on his stool and smiles, his arms open to greet me. When I don't move, he drops his arms, noticing my reaction. "I was hoping you worked tonight. You have the face of an angel."

"I've never seen you drink this much. What's going on?"

He pats the stool next to him. "Please sit with me."

I spot Stuart filling the glass bin and I take a seat. "Can I get you some coffee or water?"

"I've missed hanging out with you guys. But there's a problem I'm trying to fix." He turns, placing his knees on each side of mine, locking me in from leaving. *He has two minutes to move before I call over Stuart.*

"I'm lucky to have you guys as my friends. I hope Michael knows how lucky he is to have you, because you're not complicated, demanding, or twisted. A nice girl."

I go to move, but he tightens his legs.

"Please stay. You asked if you could help."

"Josh, what is going on? I've never seen you drink like this or act this way."

"It hasn't been work making me crazy. I've been seeing a woman who doesn't have a calm, warm, or giving bone in her body but is sexy as hell. Stupidly, I keep going back to her."

"Have you told her how you feel?"

"It doesn't matter. Her agenda is one thing and one thing only: her getting what she wants, regardless of who gets hurt. She could learn a lot from you on what a real relationship is and how to love someone other than herself."

"Do you love her?"

"No. Maybe."

"Let me get you that coffee."

He runs his hand along my thigh and squeezes to keep me from getting up. I push his hand away. "Josh, I know you're drunk and not yourself, but you have no right to act this way." I wave over Stuart.

"Jamie, is he bothering you?"

Before I can answer, I hear the voice of my rescue. "Stuart, I got her."

Michael looks at me and reaches for my hand, moving me off the stool and tucking me behind him. Then he turns his attention to Josh. "What are you doing?"

"What can I say? Your girlfriend is easy to talk to."

"I agree, but what I saw was you making her uncomfortable by not letting her leave." He puts his hand on Josh's shoulder. "Now taking into consideration you're going through some type of problem that makes you disrespect someone who is only trying to be nice to you, I will order you coffee. No more alcohol."

Josh motions a salute. "You are the boss."

"You owe Jamie an apology. I know this is the only time I will have to say anything to you about making her uncomfortable." Josh's smile faded as he looks to me standing behind Michael.

"Jamie, I am sorry for my behavior. It won't happen again."

I nod, not saying anything else. Michael takes my hand and we go upstairs to his office. I step over to the two windows that were installed after the robbery. Josh is talking with a girl and then goes to her table, taking a seat.

"That was really off. How much did you see?"

"Enough. He was one punch away from hitting the floor."

"Well I think we have done all we can for him. Now, how was your day? That is, before the flat?"

"Productive. The team decided to change the workout routine and try boxing." He pulls back his hair displaying a cut on his forehead. "I guess I didn't duck fast enough."

"Oh, you're hurt! Here, let me kiss your wound." I pull his head down to place my lips on his head. "Do you feel better?"

He points to his lips. "I might need a kiss here."

I comply with his request, leaving the situation with Josh behind and giving Michael my full attention.

*

After a few hours of bussing tables and having two glasses of tea for dinner, I need a bathroom break. I head back, hoping there's no line at the bathroom. *Oh, good two more girls and then it's my turn.* As the last one enters the bathroom, I lean against the wall and check my phone for any messages.

"Hey you." Josh is now in front of me, with one hand next to my head on the wall and the other one next to my waist. "I want to apologize again for earlier."

I can smell alcohol on his breath. "You were supposed to stop drinking."

"Girls like to buy drinks for guys too. Sweet, huh?" A girl comes out of the bathroom and I duck, but he keeps me from moving with his leg. She walks slowly by, then disappears.

I look at him and frown. "I don't need to hear anything else. Please just move."

"Jamie, we're talking." He moves a piece of hair behind my ear and I feel his other hand on my hip and that's when I react by bringing my knee up to his crotch, pushing him backwards.

"Enough!"

Michael comes flying around the corner and sees Josh bent over across from me.

"Bitch!" Josh lunges towards me but Michael pushes him back forcefully.

"I should have made you leave earlier." Josh tries to come at Michael this time, but he twists Josh's arm behind him, pushing him to the ground on his knees." He struggles to get up but Michael puts a knee in his back keeping him on the floor.

The girl who came out of the bathroom before stands now with Pete as the bouncer comes around the corner to assist Michael. "Where do you want him, boss?"

"Outside, but stay with him."

Pete speaks up. "I will call him a cab."

I address the girl. "Thank you for getting help."

"He's cute, but no one needs that drama. I'm Hannah."

"Nice to meet you. Hey, Pete—can Hannah and her friends get a round of drinks?"

"Yes, of course."

She smiles, then leaves to get her friends as Pete follows behind her.

Michael comes to me. "Sure you're alright?"

"Yes. I was done dealing with his inappropriate advances."

He laughs. "Well, he deserved the pain you inflicted. Maybe it will sober him up."

"I hope so."

*

We've stopped volunteering at Josh's company food bank and we haven't heard from him other than doors slamming from his apartment or pizza delivery for over a week. Our door is open but he has to want to talk to us, not act like he did at the bar.

But tonight, ECON is holding a fundraiser and we are attending. It calls for a formal gown, which with Meredith's help again, I found a long deep purple gown with a wide neckline that fell just off my shoulders. It fits my body snugly, with a straight skirt split just above my knee. My hair is up in a loose style with a few pieces that leaves my neck exposed. I place the last earring in my ear, then enter the living room where he is waiting for me.

I smile at the sight of him. "Loving you in this tux. Why is it guys are so sexy dressed in white and black?"

He takes my hand, spinning me around.

"You are stunning."

"Thank you. We look good together."

"That we do. Our ride is outside waiting for us."

"Let's go."

*

We walk into a charming venue with beautifully decorated tables, easels displaying upcoming projects, and music playing in the background. I was instructed to mingle and help where needed.

"I'm feeling nervous. This might be a little out of my comfort zone."

Michael places his hands on my shoulders, leaning in to kiss me, and lingers enough to help my mind slow down and my body relax. "You are good at this. Talking to people, listening to them and showing your support of the work that is done by ECON." His eyes cut to the right. "Your boss is heading this way."

I turn to greet him. "Mr. Palmer, hello."

"Ms. Morgan, I'm glad you are here."

"This is my boyfriend, Michael Tucker."

"Nice to meet you. Are you the owner/operator of 42?"

"Yes, you've heard of it?"

"My son frequented there when he attended Hopson. I have the credit card bills to prove it. You're active with the college and allocating donations to the Animal Center. Jamie will be talking to you soon about an upcoming project. I hope we can work together."

"I look forward to it."

"Jamie, your roll tonight is to mingle and introduce yourself to as many people as you can. But I want you to also have fun, because the next one you'll probably be hands-on the whole evening. Now you two eat, grab a drink, and have a good time."

"Thank you, sir."

"He seems like a nice boss unlike the one at 42," Michael remarks casually.

I squeeze his arm. "No one can top my first boss."

He smiles. "Bar?"

"After you."

With a drink in hand and two or three crab cake appetizers later, we're off meeting the invited guests. I introduce him to my co-workers and Michael introduces me to people he's worked with in the past on the council. We are a good team, moving in and out of the crowd like pros.

Heading out to the balcony for the dessert bar, the night is also cooperating with a clear sky and twinkling stars. I look over at him thinking how grateful I am to be with him. "Thank you for coming tonight."

"I wouldn't have missed it. This company means something to you and I can see it all over your face when you talk about their mission."

"Don't worry Mr. Tucker, I'm not leaving 42 yet."

He pulls me in close. "But if you choose to, I'll understand."

I lean back away from him. "I don't think I would recognize the guy you were before me. You are a respected business owner, good with people and you have a kind heart."

"Me, kind? Only because of you. I am better at honesty, trust, and love, due to how I feel about you and what I want for us."

"My responsibilities are done for tonight. It's after ten, what do you say we leave?"

"Are you sure?"

I take him by the hand. "Yes, I want you all to myself."

*

He puts his key in the door while I stand close behind him, resting my chin on his coat. The need to touch him is overtaking my proper in public thoughts and I want him out of his clothes. The door opens and he turns to pull me just inside, pressing me against the door. His lips are in pursuit of mine and I give in willingly. I slip my hands inside his coat and feel the hardness of his body while working at the buttons on his shirt, just as a group of rowdy neighbor's come by cheering us on. We stop, both of us breathing heavy, step inside and shut the door, to continue our quest of one another in private.

He's locked the door, peeled off his coat, and wraps his arms around me, catching us from falling into the table behind us.

He smiles. "I got you."

I breathlessly respond, yes you do. He slides off his shirt as my hands desperately need to touch his bare skin. I reach for his belt and undo it right before he backs me over to the sofa. We stumble hitting the arm rest falling, knocking over whatever was on the coffee table. He continues lighting up every nerve in my body and I lift my hips to help him move my dress, letting him know what I want. I feel every touch as my body collides with his. I look up at him, unsure how I ever existed without him. He whispers my name close to my ear and when the need for me takes over.

Our desire for each other grows more and more every day and tonight is no exception. He lowers himself beside me.

"Blame that on the car ride home."

I snicker. "I guess I can mark off cab curiosity."

"Yes, you can."

I kiss him. "Excuse me while I freshen up." In the bathroom, I take off my dress, tossing it out onto the bed. He follows behind me. "Miss me?" I ask playfully.

"Yes." He starts to pull the pins from my hair, wearing the smile that lights up my world every day.

"Thanks for the assistance."

"Well, I sort of messed it up with my eagerness to have you."

"Um, totally worth it."

Chapter 33

*M*ichael is reading over a paper he'd written for his morning class when I come into the living room, probably looking like a hot mess in need of some coffee. He looks over his shoulder at me. "Hey gorgeous."

I wrap my arms around his neck, kissing him. "Good morning, but I'm not sure gorgeous is the word to describe myself." I walk around the end of the sofa, plopping down next to him. "But thank you for saying it."

He sets his computer on the coffee table, pulling my legs into his lap. "I remember these legs from last night." I lean up to kiss him. "Aww yes, I remember these lips as well. I enjoyed our after-party. I think I last looked at the clock about 3:45."

"We were a little crazy about each other last night. Where is the lamp we knocked over?"

"In the trash. We did well not to break more." He kisses my knee.

"You in a tux. Irresistible."

"I made some coffee. I also cleaned up from our food attack. Especially the honey off the counter." He smiles, raising an eyebrow at me.

"You started the honey dripping."

"It looked good drizzled all over you. Are you still sticky? Let me check." He grabs at my shirt.

"No sir, you have a paper due this morning, remember?"

"I do, but…"

He is grabbing at me and I am playfully fighting him off, but we both know breakfast will have to wait.

*

March brings windy, chilly days on campus, which call for warm clothes or nights like last night. I'm down on the floor looking for my shoe when I hear Michael come into my room.

"May I help?"

I get up, pulling on my shoe. "Found it!"

"It's cold outside. Maybe we should stay in today."

I kiss him. "I want to stay and cozy up with you too." I pick up my backpack and grab my phone out of the purse from last night and notice I have messages.

"Hold on and let me check these. Oh my God!"

"What is it?"

"Caleb was in an accident! He's in the hospital."

"Is he okay?"

"I don't know. He asked if I would come see him, but that was hours ago."

"I can drop you off and then drop off my paper. Try and call him."

My Heart

Michael takes my backpack while I try to call the hospital.

"I was able to reach the nurses' station, but he's getting an X-ray. Hopefully by the time I get to his room, he'll be back."

*

The door to his room is half open, so I knock. "Caleb?"

"Jamie, come in." His leg is immobilized.

"What happened to you? I just got your messages."

"How was the fundraiser?"

"It was great, but tell me what happened to you."

"I went out last night with some friends to Georgios for pizza. We decided to go catch a movie. We paid the bill and went outside. We walked to the corner of Main and South Street and there were people everywhere, due to the concert at Wickham Hall. We stepped off the curb and then out of nowhere, a faded red pickup truck plowed into all of us crossing the street. Unfortunately for my group, we were among the people up front."

"Who else got hurt?"

"Steve fractured his hand when he caught himself from hitting the pavement. Phillip had some bruises and a cut above his right eye."

"Did anyone get the license number or were they caught?"

"My dad told me it was found abandoned three blocks over."

"A witness from the coffee shop said it sped up before plowing into us. I think you know what I'm about to say."

"You're thinking it was Stacey."

"I haven't seen her anywhere. Think about it. A black SUV almost ran you and Michael over, then the break-in at your apartment, not to mention the phone calls you've been getting. Plus she has not been seen lately. You and Michael need to be careful."

"Maybe the drugs are getting to you. Is there anything I can do before I go?"

"No. Promise me you will be careful." He takes my hand. "Talk to Michael, tell him what I said."

I bend over to kiss his cheek. "Text me about your surgery because we'll come back."

Slipping out into the hallway, his words are still with me. Could Stacey be the cause behind all that is happening? Is she capable? I haven't seen her, but I thought she finally realized how crazy she's been and backed off.

I text Michael that I would explain everything later. Then walking back to campus, I decide to go to the Registrar's office to check on the name of a past student. I have been thinking about it lately and maybe it's time find out about her.

The lady who greets me stands behind a long counter. "May I help you?"

I ask her to look up a female student with the last name Artosa. She types, but finds nothing. No one currently attending in the computer by that name."

"Is it possible to check maybe as far back as three years?"

She punches away on the computer again but comes up with nothing. "I'm sorry dear but I really can't give you much information even if she was in our system without written authorization."

"Thank you for your help. I might have the spelling wrong."

"Well you can go the library and check a few things, but without knowing more I won't be able to help you."

"Thank you for your time."

Maybe now is not the time to open a brand new mystery. My life is so good just as it is. I don't have to follow the wishes of my dad and find this girl. At least not now.

*

Standing at the coffee counter I'm thinking of Caleb and what he said not realizing Michael is now standing next to me.

"Hey, are you okay?"

I look at him then shake my head. "Yeah my mind is elsewhere. How did you know I was here?"

"Your backpack has a pink peony flower hanging on it and you are wearing your blue coat. What are you thinking about that has you so distracted."

My name is called. "Do you want something?"

He looks at the guy behind the counter then back at me. "Morning Nate. I will take a bottle of water."

Nate tosses it to Michael. "Good luck this coming week."

"Hey, you too." Placing the water in his pocket and my hand in his, we start walking to my next class, but veer off to the left.

"Where are we going? My class is that way?"

"Let's go to the fountain."

"What's going on with you?"

"I just want time with my girl and then we'll get you off to your class on time."

We grab a bench, sitting close as he blocks the wind away from me.

"Do you think after our honeymoon dating is done that we'll lose this connection?"

"Not if I have a say." He waves his hand between us. "This will never change because our relationship has gone to a level of no return. You and I are destined."

"This is true." I kiss him. "I've been thinking about my summer work schedule. I'm not going to take classes because I want my free time to be with you. Maybe do some traveling. We can go to the beach or the mountains. I even checked into some mini trips like kayaking or hiking."

"I would love to do all of that with you."

"Then it's set. My graduation gift to you will be trips. Just keep in mind it won't be as nice as Colorado."

"I am up for whatever."

"If we go to the beach we can eat crab, drink beer, and relax in a hammock. We can watch the sun set, walk on the beach, and live out of backpacks."

"You in a bikini with sun-kissed skin makes for a pretty good trip to me. I will enjoy anything you plan. But you are not telling me everything."

"Today I decided to go by the registrar's office and ask about the name, Artosa. But she didn't find anything, not even a few years back. Maybe I have the spelling wrong."

"There are other ways to find this girl."

"Maybe, but for now I'm going to drop it. It's not big on my priority list of things to do, but maybe someday. My father wanted us to find each other. I think I need more time."

"It will always be your decision if you find her or not. I support you either way."

"What do you think about Caleb's accident? I mean it's very similar to ours."

"Are you thinking it could be Stacey?"

"I don't want to think she could go to this extreme, but now I'm not sure."

"I agree. But for right now, can I say how much last night meant to me?"

I giggle at his sweetness. "You could show me."

He wraps me up in his arms and my nose touches his neck. "You smell so good." My phone vibrates almost breaking the hold he has on me.

I ignore the interruption and only concentrate on him. He is right. We are forever and always and the world can wait. My phone alerts me to a message. He touches my chin with his finger.

"You want to look at it? It might be Caleb."

Letting out a sigh, I do. "It's a message from Stacey." I put it on speaker, so he can hear what she has to say.

"Hey, Jamie I want to clear the air between us. I've been soul searching lately and realize I've not been the nicest person to you. I want to bury the bad stuff and move on. Maybe all of us can be friends sometime in the future so I need to start with you. Please meet me tonight at 8:00 in Dot's café. Just us girls. Hope you come, Stacey."

He sits up, leaning his elbows on his knees, and looks down at the sidewalk. "I don't think she has an apologetic bone in her body."

"Maybe she discovered that she burned all her bridges and wants to leave Hopson with a clear conscience."

"You shouldn't meet with her. What if Caleb is right about her or we are right and she's to blame for things that have occurred recently? I don't want to risk your safety for the sake of finding out why she feels different now."

I lean my head against his arm. "I'm not trying to take chances or put myself in harm's way, but if closure comes from meeting her, then I think I should. Besides you can be there right after practice. Ask Dottie if you can slip in the back of the café."

He turns his head to me, his face clearly concerned. "I'll be there by 7:45. You show up right at 8:00."

"Fair enough."

"Oh, I almost forgot." He pulls a piece of yarn from his pocket. "The Life Studies class is making these to promote health and happiness. May I have your wrist?"

He slides it on, pulling it closed. It's made out of red, yellow, and orange string looped with a small bar that says, "Forever."

"It's sweet. You are my forever." We kiss. "I don't want to go but..."

"Let's go. I said you would make it on time." He pulls me up and we walk until the sidewalk ends, holding on to each other just a few more minutes. He pulls me in for a kiss. "I love you."

I smile, looking up at him. "See you at 8:00." I walk away from him backwards, pointing at my new bracelet. I say it where anyone around us can hear: "I love you Michael Tucker!" He places his hand over his heart and when I reach the door of my next class, I turn to see him still looking at me. I wave to him and then he turns to walk away.

Chapter 34

*T*wo classes later I'm thinking of my time by the fountain with Michael as I enter the apartment. I can't wait to start planning his graduation trip to the beach as my fingers run over the bracelet. Heading into the kitchen for a banana, I step out onto the balcony to breathe in the fresh air as I listen to the trees rustle from the wind. I think of all the time I've spent doubting myself, or thinking that love would elude me, when it just needed the right place, the right person, and trust.

Back in the living room, I check my phone. One text from Susan. I'll call her back later tonight—she stays up late and we can catch up then. There's also a text from Ruby, stating she sent me a care package. I place the phone on the table, then head to the bathroom before leaving for the meeting with Stacey. Seeing the purple dress reminds me to drop it off at the dry cleaners tomorrow and buy a new lamp. I can hear my phone vibrating when I remember where it is. I run out reaching for it, when I catch a glimpse of a figure standing a few steps from the closed door in the darkness of the hall.

"Hey, babe. You couldn't wait until eight, could you?" I look at the phone seeing Susan's number, but it goes to voicemail. I missed it again. I turn to the door where he's still standing. Michael?"

Still no movement. I realize this is not Michael. His body is stiff with arms hanging straight down wearing gloves and dressed in dark clothes. Panic rips through my body as I take off to my room, but I'm grabbed by my hoodie, and fall to the floor on my back. I hit my head hard against the floor and drop my phone. I try to get up, but I'm pulled around to face the person who has a mask over his face.

My Heart

He towers over me but I start my attempt to get up. He quickly covers my mouth, but I wiggle free and try again screaming out for help. This time he hits me on the left side of my face, forcing my body away from him, and sending me banging into the back of the sofa. Seconds go by as he stands behind me breathing heavily, saying nothing. I reach for a pillow to swing at him, but he swats it away and grabs me by the waist pulling me up against him while his other gloved hand covers my face. I can't breathe; I tear at his hand and kick with everything I have, but there's something on the cloth over my face. I claw at it, losing my ability to fight back as my arms drop, limp by my side. He drags me towards the bedroom kicking the door shut behind us.

*

My eyes open and I blink to clear my vision. I'm lying on the floor on my stomach and all I can see are two black boots next to me. My head feels heavy but when I try to push up, his foot comes down on my back. I yell. "What do you want?"

He bends down next to me, rubbing his hand over my hair sending chills up my spine, then covers my mouth and nose as I try and scream but my words are muffled. I start choking, losing the ability to move once again. I lay limp on the floor, my breathing steady, and my eyes slowly shut. I picture Michael this afternoon when he gave me the bracelet, his fingers touching the word, "Forever." I blink a couple of times as the beats of my heart slow down, easing my body into a sleep as I hold Michael's image. But just like me, he fades away.

Epilogue...

My arms are wrapped around her as we lay together, and I watch her fingers make circles on my skin. My beautiful girl means everything to me. Could I love her any deeper than I do now?

"Hey mister, what are you thinking?"

"About you in your dress tonight. You took my breath away."

"I hoped you would like it."

"The cab ride home proved how much."

"Who knew we could be this in love?"

"I did."

"You always believed in us."

"Yes."

"I remember the first day we met when you opened the door I thought you were perfect. I couldn't think or speak and was jealous that Michaela had you as a boyfriend. Once I regained my composure and you invited me in, I immediately felt safe, calm and home. When I left Texas, I was scared and thought I was destined to be unhappy in life." I poke his arm with my finger. *"But the way I feel now is so different."*

"Tell me."

"You opened yourself up for me which brought me back to life. I'm not scared anymore because I found love with you."

He slides me down onto my back, keeping eye contact and traces my cheek with his thumb. His eyes narrow and he smiles. My hand comes up to touch his perfectly scruffy face and he leaves a soft kiss on my palm.

My Heart

"Michael, you are my heart."

*

I am awakened by a knock on my bedroom door. I don't want to open my eyes because she is so clear—from the smell of flowers on her skin to the feel of her body next to mine I hold onto to her as long as I can.

"Michael. Your dad is here, and we need to talk with you."

I force my eyes open, swinging my legs over the side of the bed. I sit up, not wanting to lose the dream. The accident left me with a deep laceration on my arm, bruising, and a broken wrist but nothing hurts as much as missing her. "I'll be out in a minute."

"Alright."

I go into the bathroom, turning on the water. As I reach for my toothbrush, I see Jamie's still in the holder next to mine. I look up in the mirror seeing weeks of growth on my face and don't remember the last time I showered. Out of nowhere, I hit the wall next to the mirror with my fist, then again, this time knocking it loose from the wall. I scream something that comes from my gut and pull it off the wall, throwing it into my bedroom. Next the shower curtain...anything I can put my hands on lands in the floor or tub. I slide to the floor, cupping my hands to my head. Crying is not something I ever did, but every day since she's been missing, my whole body aches, I'm angry at the police, but angrier at myself for not being able to protect her. I pick up her toothbrush holding it in my hand.

My dad comes to the bathroom door, viewing the damage I just inflicted. "Michael come with me. Let's leave the apartment." He touches my arm.

I shake my head. "I can't. I need to be here, someone needs to be here."

259

"Michael, please."

"No! Everyone wants me to believe she is gone but she's not. I saw her in the car with Josh, yelling my name with her hands pressed against the glass. She was pleading for my help."

"But the police found nothing at the crash site. No sign of Jamie at all."

I look up at my mom. "She wouldn't just leave me. Something is keeping her from me or she's hurt."

My mom starts to cry. "Harrison, help him back to the bed."

"Son, your hand is bleeding. Laura, go find something to clean him up." She leaves and he helps me sit on the bed. "You need to eat. If you're sick, you can't help Jamie."

Mom returns, standing in front of me as she cleans off the cuts on my hand. I look at her wiping tears off her own face, which makes me realize we have all been affected.

My dad stands. "You are in love with a woman who vanished, and no one can explain to you where she is or what happened. She would not have left you if there wasn't a damn good reason. Trust your gut. You have unlimited resources to help in your search. I just need to know what we can do to help."

At that moment Harrison Tucker is the dad I need. He knows I won't give up, no matter what the police have said. He is with me now, backing my decision.

"Mom, how about some food?" She smiles, finishes my hand and then leaves the room.

"You know that is probably the best thing you could have done for her."

"It's hard to see her upset. I'm going to shower." My father looks at my bathroom. "I'll go to Jamie's room and use hers." I grab some clothes, then look back at him. "I guess I'll call Ruby and Susan to check in with them."

"Good idea." I go to leave and hear him exhale.

I stop. "Thanks for your support. It means a lot." He smiles.

I walk into her room, wanting to see her, but only find the purple dress she wore to the fundraiser laying across the bed. After the police cleared the apartment of any clues, my mother came in and straightened up the room. I touch the material, thinking back on that night then go into her bathroom. I step inside the shower and let the water hit my skin for the first time in weeks. Then I place my hands on the tiles, letting my head be covered with the hot water. I will keep her tucked in my heart until the day she is found and releases me to love her and only her again.

Thank you for reading "My Heart" and look for the sequel, "Release My Heart" available at the end of 2018.

I want to extend my thanks and love to the following:

Thank you to my patient and understanding husband that sat back and watched me take this journey not knowing where it was going to take us. My dream came true because of your love and support. You are my heart! I love you!!

Thanks to Amy, my beautiful daughter. Thank you for helping me achieve my dream and answering my many questions about the computer, photos and book cover. You helped me more than you think, but always do. I love you!

Thank you to my son, Taylor. You helped to get my thoughts in order at the beginning and encouraged me to write my way. Thank you for always asking, "Are you done yet?" I can finally say, yes I am! I love you!

Thank you to my sister, Cheryl. You helped in putting many words into a readable form, you supported my breakdowns and just listened when I needed to talk. Thank you for always encouraging and believing one day I would get here. I love you!

Thanks to Genna for giving me your valuable input on the story when it was new, for proofing and being sweet to listen to me talk about it over and over. I love you!

Thanks to my mom, Shirley for reading it at 76 and enjoying the story. Love ya!

Thanks to Christine and Ashley for proofreading and your comments and concerns.

Thanks to Alexis for promotional pictures. I appreciate all you have done!

Thanks to Philip Andrews Photography for the Author headshots and making it fun!

Thanks to Meg Reid for the beautiful book cover and Amy Elizabeth Bishop for editing.

Thanks to Tieka for reading it at the beginning and for your encouragement and kind words. Now write that children's book!

Thanks Terry for reading it when it was all kinds of crazy and sharing the love of reading!

68689070R00150